Taking Time

Legacy Series, Book 4

PAULA KAY

DEDICATION

To Diane and Ed.
Thank you for sharing your love
and passion for Guatemala with me.

TABLE OF CONTENTS

CHAPTER 1

The silence in the room was almost more than Gigi could bear. She could count on one hand the number of arguments that she'd had with Douglas in the four years that they'd been married. She looked at him now across the room where he stood staring out the window towards the garden and the view of the bridge beyond. She loved him so much. Who would have ever thought that the love of her life would be right under her nose for all these years?

Arianna had known.

Gigi smiled in spite of the tension she was still feeling. She still missed Arianna so much at times. It had been five years since the young girl's death, and the truth was that time was making it better—easier, she supposed. But it still overwhelmed her—still threatened her with that lost feeling of not quite knowing what her life was going to be about now.

She turned her attention towards Douglas, who was crossing the room towards her, looking every bit as unhappy as what Gigi was feeling about their argument.

"Honey."

He reached out to pull her towards him and she stepped away, resisting the embrace that she normally fell into so easily.

"Douglas, please. I know that look. Don't patronize me."

Even to her own ear, her words sounded too harsh. It was not what he was doing. She knew better than that. He was a good man, loving and generous with his affection for her—something she appreciated so much about him and their relationship. She knew that she'd been difficult to please lately, to understand. Heck, she was so confused herself that she really couldn't seem to put her general feelings of discontent into words most of the time. She just knew that something was wrong. Something was missing.

Douglas gave her a look as he pulled her to him, just forceful enough that she conceded as she eased back against his chest, feeling his kiss on her cheek before he spoke again into her ear.

"You know I'm trying to understand—to figure out what it is that will make you happy, love."

Gigi sighed as she turned to face him. "I know, honey. I do know that." She willed herself to smile, to reassure him that everything would be okay. If only she felt more confident about this herself. She took a deep breath before trying again. "I just don't understand the big deal about my getting a job. You know how much I enjoyed taking care of Arianna—of the Sinclair family. Douglas, it's all I've ever known and I'm just feeling so—so bored without anything to do. And if I'm being honest, it's weird for me—having these other people around that you've hired." She felt her position growing stronger as she continued. She had a right to make some of these decisions for them—for herself. She was a confident woman and it was time to start thinking about what she really needed to be happy.

"But I only want to take care of you—to give you some of the comforts that you've provided for others over the years—for you to finally take some time for yourself. You deserve that, honey. And we both agreed that this retirement was going to stick, right?"

He was teasing her now, but she knew that it was nearly as hard for him as it was for her since he'd retired this past year, something that had been pushed off more times than he'd likely admit before he finally took the plunge himself. She'd gotten to know him quite well since they'd been married, and she had an inkling that his almost daily tee times at the local golf club were becoming a bit boring to him.

"We did agree, yes." She was smiling at him despite the irritation she still felt. "Maybe a part-time job, though, for me? Just something to occupy a bit of my day."

"But then what about our travels? I just don't want you to feel tied down—us to feel tied down. What about a little trip? We've not been to Lia and Antonio's—to Italy yet this year. I'm sure she'd love to have us. And we could spend more time with your family."

Gigi knew that he was trying hard to please her but deep down, as much as she loved their visits to Italy, she knew that it was going to take more than a trip to ease this feeling she'd been having lately.

"No, not now. I do want to go back this year, but I don't think it's what I—what we need right now. I don't know, Douglas. Honestly, I'm not trying to drive you crazy. I promise. I just can't shake this feeling I've been having lately. I guess unlike most people, retirement really does not agree with me, does it?" She laughed then, trying to lighten the mood and wanting their argument to be over. She hated fighting with Douglas.

She'd sort out for herself what needed to be done, even if that meant keeping the appointment she had scheduled with the agency in the city. She had a good reputation with them, and she knew that finding a job would be as easy as reactivating her application on file. She felt bad even thinking about doing it behind Douglas's back, especially knowing how he felt about it, but after their argument it felt more important than ever that she was able to make some decisions for herself right now. Besides, she was never going to be truly happy unless she figured out a cure for this unsettled feeling she'd been having. She knew that he would understand eventually.

Douglas pulled her close for another hug. "We'll be okay. I promise you're going to get used to having me around. And you know the invitation to let me teach you the joys of golfing remains open." He laughed as she eyed him with skepticism.

"What, and spoil your time with the boys? I don't think so."

Gigi really had no interest in playing golf, and she was fine with the fact that it got Douglas out of the house for several hours during the day. It allowed her some time to get together with her friends; and as much as she was happy to have him home more than when he was working all of the long hours in the law office, she suspected that too much time together might not be as good for them as she'd once imagined.

She turned to give him a quick kiss on the lips. "We'll talk more about this later." She needed to make it clear that he didn't necessarily have the final word in the matter.

He nodded and she knew that they'd be okay—for now.

"Okay, hon. Now let's talk about some dinner. What are you making for me, woman?" He swatted her on the rear playfully.

"Hey, now. You know that I've gotten really good with a couple of things I've learned from Lia and Chase." She laughed at the standing joke that was her lack of skills in the kitchen.

"I'm not complaining at all. You can delight me with your gourmet Italian surprises any night of the week."

Gigi giggled in response. waiting for him to continue. "But?"

"But I didn't notice anything being readied in the kitchen, so how about if I take you to that new Mexican place that just opened? I've read some good reviews about it and I think we could both use a margarita." He winked.

"That sounds great. As does a pitcher of margaritas." Gigi laughed as she walked across the room. "Let me just change clothes and I'll see you downstairs in a minute."

Gigi stared at her reflection in the bathroom mirror, willing herself not to cry. She wasn't okay. She really wasn't. She could put on a good show, and she didn't want Douglas to worry about her so much. It wasn't his fault, even though she wished it were as easy as letting him fix things. Maybe it was time for her to seek a little therapy. She'd never done it in her life, but she'd seen how positive it had been for Arianna as she was going through her most difficult times. And Douglas had shared with her what it had meant to him after the passing of his wife. Gigi was a bit old-school in terms of thinking that she could overcome her emotions, but she couldn't pretend that she wasn't facing some sort of crisis. And she knew enough about depression to know that it was something she needed to get a handle on earlier rather than later.

She quickly changed her clothes, splashed some cold water on her face, and dabbed on just a hint of make-up. She'd suck it up for now, trying to have a "normal" night out with her husband. They had so much to be grateful for. She needed to remember that above all else.

PAULA KAY

CHAPTER 2

Gigi was humming to herself in the kitchen when she heard Douglas making his way down the steps. She had woken up feeling determined to extend the wonderful time that the two of them had shared the night before—to put any arguments they'd been having behind them and start working on resolving some of these strange feelings she'd been having lately.

She smiled as she felt Douglas's arms around her and the quick peck of his lips against her cheek.

"Good morning, love. Something smells delicious in here. Do you have one of those scones for me?"

"I do. Yes." Gigi smiled in response. "Why don't you have a seat and I'll pour you a cup of coffee?"

"Sorry, no can do. I have a tee time in thirty minutes. But if you'd make me a cup to go, I'd be ever so appreciative."

"Sure, honey."

Gigi leaned over to return a kiss to his cheek before she grabbed a coffee mug out of the cupboard.

"What do you have going on today?" Douglas asked

as he took the coffee from her.

"Oh I don't know. Some shopping maybe, and I'm going to see if Evelyn is available for lunch. It's been so long since the two of us have had a proper chat and I'm feeling a bit guilty about that."

Evelyn was one of Gigi's best friends, who'd been in her life for all of the years that she'd worked for the Sinclairs—more than twenty-five years in total that they'd known one another. She, like Gigi, had worked as a housekeeper or nanny and for just as many years as Gigi had been in the business, and typically they had lots to talk about and so much in common.

Lately, though, Gigi had felt a bit of distance between them—if she was being honest, she'd felt that from several of her friends. She suspected it was due to the change in her lifestyle—the inheritance and her marriage to Douglas—but she didn't want to believe that her friendships were as fragile as that.

She sighed. She didn't think that she'd changed—that the money had changed her. But there were differences. She wasn't naive enough to think that there wouldn't be. It was one of the things that she'd been struggling with, for sure. Trying to blend her old, working life with her new, wealthy retired life. She'd like to believe that it was possible. She'd do her best to make it all work and with her old relationships intact.

"Hello? Earth to my lovely."

Douglas was pulling her towards him, laughing as he

did so.

"Oh, sorry, darling. What were you saying?"

"I was just wishing you a great day and thanking you for my breakfast."

She saw that he'd picked up the scone she'd left for him from the table, but had added one more to it.

"Douglas. How about a banana instead of that second scone?" She laughed because she didn't want to appear the nagging wife, but they'd both decided after their last physical that they wanted to each drop ten pounds or so.

Douglas looked thoughtful for a minute before he put the extra scone back on the tray and accepted the banana that Gigi was offering him. "Okay, you win this time."

They both laughed and Douglas pulled Gigi to him one more time.

"Are we okay, honey? After yesterday, I mean."

Gigi looked into his eyes and nodded. "Yes, we're okay."

"Good, because you know how much I adore you, my love. I don't want you to be unhappy for one second because of me." He looked intently back at her before kissing her on the lips.

God, but he still took her breath away every time he kissed her like that. How could she have been so lucky? She needed to remember this every day—to count her blessings, and Douglas being the very best thing to have ever happened to her.

"I adore you too, honey. Really." She looked at him,

willing him to feel the deep emotion of her words. "Now scoot. Or you're going to be late for your golf date."

After Douglas left, Gigi tidied up the kitchen before Nathalie arrived. Finally, at Douglas's insistence, they'd hired the young girl to come in for the mornings to do the cleaning and laundry. But it wasn't something that Gigi was comfortable with and she had yet to just not clean up after herself. She doubted that this was something that would ever change. She smiled as she thought about how ridiculous it all seemed—her having a housekeeper. She'd probably need to talk to Douglas about it, but now she felt somewhat obligated to the girl over the job. She sighed thinking about it as she made her way to the laundry room to get started with some folding.

A few minutes later she heard Nathalie letting herself in the front door.

"Nat? I'm in the laundry room."

"What are you doing in there?" The young girl laughed and Gigi knew that she was well aware of Gigi's resistance to having her there to look after them. God, she must take the prize for the best boss ever.

She couldn't help but giggle as she thought about how tough Mrs. Sinclair had been on her when she'd just started with them. She was very demanding, and it took a few years for their relationship to really develop. Gigi knew that she would have quit very early on, but once they'd brought Arianna home, her fate with the family had been sealed. The infant had melted her heart the first time she'd held her, and Gigi knew that they needed her then. She would become the child's nanny and her life would never be the same.

She wiped the tear away from her face just as Nathalie entered the room.

"What are you doing in here, Gigi? Honestly, why don't you let me do that?" She reached to pull the towel that Gigi was folding out of her hands.

Gigi relented, taking a seat on the nearby chair to watch Nathalie as she folded the towels. "Okay, okay. I didn't really have much else to do, so I figured I'd get a start on it for you."

"Well, I do appreciate that, but some days you leave so little for me to do around here that I'm starting to feel guilty over it."

"Oh, don't feel guilty Nat. Please. Honestly, you're terrific." Gigi stood up to give the young girl a swift hug.

"Well, you and Mr. Jackson are by far the best employers I've ever had." She laughed. "I don't know how the heck I got so lucky finding this job—finding the two of you."

"We feel lucky to have found you too. How about if I leave you to fold this load and then you come join me in the kitchen for a cup of coffee? I want to hear all about your date last night." Gigi winked at the young girl.

She'd been living somewhat vicariously through her ever since Nathalie had started with them six months ago.

Their friendship was fast and easy, and Gigi appreciated the distraction of the exciting life that their housekeeper seemed to be living in the city. In some ways, she supposed that Nathalie reminded her of Arianna—at least before the accident—and before she'd gotten sick. The Arianna of those days was full of spunk and always the life of a party.

Gigi left to go to the kitchen, glancing at the time. She'd have one last cup of coffee and a nice chat with Nathalie before she'd go upstairs to try to give Lia a call in Italy. They'd been playing phone tag, and she had a strong feeling that talking to her good friend might help with some of the feelings she'd been having.

Lia and Gigi had been through a lot together since Lia had come back into Arianna's life. Everything that happened after Arianna met her birth mom had been intense, and ultimately Gigi and Lia had become the best of friends, sharing a similar grief for the young girl who'd left their lives way too soon.

Gigi found herself wondering why her mind seemed to be filled with so many thoughts lately about Arianna— about that time. It wasn't that it was uncommon for her to be reminded of Arianna, but lately she was feeling a familiar feeling of dread—of sadness.

Gigi and Nathalie enjoyed their coffee together before Gigi sent the girl off to collect the ingredients for an Italian dinner that she herself planned to cook for Douglas that night.

CHAPTER 3

Gigi made her way upstairs to the master bedroom. It still seemed odd to her, even after five years, to be sleeping in this room—to call it her own. It was the very same room that she'd cleaned for more than twenty years while working for the Sinclairs, and she didn't know if she'd ever truly consider it her own. But Arianna had been so insistent about leaving Gigi the house, and she knew how much it pleased the young girl to think of giving it to her.

After much discussion, she and Douglas had decided to keep the house and live there together after they'd been married, but Douglas had assured Gigi that Arianna had made it clear to him that she was to do with it as she saw fit—that she could sell the house if she wanted to. Arianna wanted Gigi to be happy and to have the home and the money, to able to retire and travel or whatever it was that she wanted to do.

Lately, she really had been having second thoughts about living in the big house, but until she had a better idea of what the future would hold, they'd stay put. There were too many memories here to just let it go so easily, but Gigi had the feeling the time was coming.

She settled into the chaise lounge with her phone. It was her favorite place to sit and rest during the day when she was alone, either reading or sipping her tea as she enjoyed the spectacular view of the Golden Gate Bridge from the large bay windows. She pulled up Lia's number, hoping that she'd catch her friend at home for the evening.

"Pronto?"

Gigi smiled when she heard her friend's familiar greeting on the other end of the phone.

"Lia, it's Gigi. I'm so happy that I caught you at home."

"Gigi, finally. I've been dying to talk to you. How are you?"

Gigi felt instantly better at the sound of her friend's voice. No matter what was happening in their lives, the two seemed to share a special connection. Gigi was a full ten years older than Lia, but their common Italian heritage and their shared loved of Arianna had bonded them in ways in which Gigi hadn't connected with other women in her life before.

"Si," Gigi answered, "I'm doing fine—well, maybe not so fine exactly, but first I want to hear about you—all the good news, please. How's everything going with Antonio? Do you still feel like you're on your honeymoon?" Gigi laughed, knowing that her friend would be blushing on the other end of the line.

Lia and Antonio had been married for a year and a half, and Gigi had rarely seen a couple as happy or more in love than they were. Their courtship had been quite romantic, and she knew that Lia felt more than grateful at the way fate had brought her back with Arianna's birth father—after so many years, after so many things had happened.

"Si, I do in fact feel like I am still in my honeymoon phase, thank you very much. Antonio promises me that I will feel like that every day, so we shall see. How about you and Douglas? I learned from watching you two lovebirds, you know." Lia laughed, and Gigi flashed to the memory of her wedding in the garden—how wonderful it had been having all her friends there.

"Oh, Douglas is fine. You know, we're both still struggling a bit trying to figure out what the heck to do with our lives, but overall things are mostly fine between us." Gigi knew, even as she was speaking, that it wasn't going to go over with Lia. She knew Gigi too well not to recognize when she was trying to sugarcoat something.

"Okay. Spill it, friend. What do you mean by mostly fine? Is everything okay between you and Douglas?"

"We're fine. We'll be fine. Just been having a little clash lately. Nothing that we won't work out, or that's wrong between us necessarily—just him trying to make me happy. But we're okay. Honestly."

"So, what's the clash about?"

"Well, I know it's no surprise to you that I've been feeling a bit off center for a while now—really, since Arianna passed away if I'm being honest. Things have been good with Douglas—our courtship certainly was a good distraction, but you know that suddenly not working was a hard thing for me."

"Yes, I do know that."

It had been a hard time for Lia too—after Arianna had died. It was another thing that the two women had had in common—the suddenness of having the money that Arianna had left them, of not having to work for other people, other families—this had been Lia's profession also before she'd met Arianna—and she'd had a very rough time during her own transition and move to Tuscany.

The line went quiet for just a moment, and Gigi knew that Lia was waiting for her to continue.

"We had an argument the other day because I brought up the idea of getting a part-time job with a family again."

"Ah, okay."

Gigi felt that she heard an instant understanding in her friend's response.

"I really don't see what the big deal is with it, but Douglas seems to think that my taking a job means that he's not taking good care of me or something. He doesn't get that I appreciate everything he's wanting to do for me.

I do. But I still need to be able to make some decisions about my own life. Does that make sense?"

"It does. Yes." Lia laughed lightly. "These macho men in our lives who feel this crazy need to provide. Sometimes I don't get it myself. But on the other hand, I mostly really like it—once I learned how to adjust to the sentiment behind it all. And I know how much Douglas loves you, Gigi. I'm sure that his heart is in the right place."

"Oh, I know that it is. He just doesn't understand why I'd want to continue working at all. But he should understand, really. I mean, it did take him a while—as you know—to be able to finally retire from his own job and stop working so much. And honestly, I think the man is probably getting a little bored with his day-to-day golfing and the few other things that he's got going on too, so I guess this is partly my frustration with it all."

"Okay. So is it really that you want to be working again? Or that you're just not sure what it is you should be doing?"

Lia's question was right on, and exactly vocalized Gigi's frustration with her own confusion about the way she'd been feeling.

Gigi was trying to keep from crying but she knew that her emotion was going to be apparent when she spoke. But it was why she'd phoned her friend. She needed someone to talk to, and Lia had always been there for her.

"I don't know, Lia." She cried openly. "I don't know

if I want a job at all. I just know that I'm feeling very bored and like I'm only half here sometimes. It's really not Douglas. I thank God every day that I do have him or I'd probably drive myself crazy. I'm—I'm just not so sure that we want the same things right now. This idea of being retired—of being able to travel whenever the mood strikes us. The idea of it sounds nice, but the reality is that I'm—I'm feeling kind of empty inside. Does that make sense?"

"Yes, it does. I was about to ask you if you wanted to come here for a while. Both of you, of course, are invited anytime you like. I think you know that. But it sounds like that might fit into the category of something you are not wanting right now."

"Well, I had thought about that. That maybe I could come help you out at the restaurant for a while. Despite my horrible start at cooking, I have learned a thing or two from you and I know that I'd enjoy learning more."

The two women laughed at Gigi's comment.

"And maybe Douglas would enjoy spending time with Antonio at the vineyard. It really is so lovely there. Oh, I don't know. I guess if I'm being honest, my heart tells me that another trip to Italy is not the answer—not that I don't always adore spending time with you, or that we won't be up for a visit soon. I just feel like there's something else that I need to figure out, and a trip to Italy right now feels a bit like running away from that."

"I understand all of that," Lia said, and Gigi believed

her.

Lia had gone through a lot of soul-searching herself during the years following Arianna's death, and Gigi knew that she could relate to her on many levels.

"I do have an appointment with the agency in the city this afternoon which I think I should keep. I'll just go in and have a chat with them—see what they have available for part-time positions right now."

"That sounds like a good idea. Who knows? Maybe they have some type of temporary position that would be a good compromise for both you and Douglas right now," Lia said. "Does he know that you are going in for the meeting?"

"No, he doesn't. And I'm not really happy keeping it from him. When I brought up the idea, he had such a strong opinion about it that I didn't want to discuss the appointment I'd already set up. I figure I'll tell him after I hear what they have to say. As much as his resistance frustrates me, I wouldn't take a job without speaking to him about it—without making sure we were both in agreement, at least somewhat."

"It sounds like maybe you'll have a better idea after the meeting. I say to trust yourself in the decision. And if it's what is really going to make you happy, I find it hard to believe that Douglas wouldn't support it. He'll come around. And I'm sure everything's going to be fine."

"Thanks so much for the support. I already feel a lot better after talking to you."

"Any time, my friend. Please do let me know how the meeting goes and what you end up deciding."

Gigi clicked off the phone feeling better about her meeting in a couple hours. She'd try to just relax about everything. She was only collecting information at this point. Nothing more. And Lia was right. She did know that eventually everything was going to be okay.

CHAPTER 4

Gigi sat in the lobby at the agency downtown, waiting for her meeting with Anna. She was quite early, so she had a few minutes to collect her thoughts. Being here reminded of that time so long ago when she'd first heard about the job with the Sinclair family. There was a small circle among the domestic staff in the area, so she'd known that a few of her friends had already interviewed for the position and none of them had had any good things to say about Mrs. Sinclair, the lady of the house. But Gigi had been out of work for a while and she really needed the money that the full-time job promised.

She remembered the interview well. The Sinclairs had been living in the city at the time and she instantly took a liking to Mr. Sinclair. He seemed much more easygoing and friendly than his wife, but it was clear to Gigi that she was the one who ruled the house. She was the one who would be making the decision as to whether or not Gigi would be a fit.

Gigi remembered leaving that interview feeling like

she'd blown it, only to be called a few hours later by the agency, telling her that the job was hers if she wanted it. She moved in to start work right away and the first few months were difficult, but then they adopted Arianna and everything changed. Gigi was destined to be there for that family, to see them through everything over the years. And though Mrs. Sinclair never totally eased up on her, over time they had an understanding and it worked for them.

Gigi's thoughts were interrupted by the ding of her phone, alerting her to a text message.

Darling, on my way home. See you soon? xo

Douglas. Just like that, she felt a pang of guilt for being there without his knowing. No matter about their argument or how much his viewpoint of her working was frustrating her, she didn't like keeping secrets from him. She bit her bottom lip as she considered how to respond to him.

Honey, I decided to keep a meeting at the agency but I won't make any decisions without discussing with you first, okay? Be home in an hour or so. Please don't be mad. xo

She waited for the alert to come, wondering how upset he'd be about the meeting, when Anna came out to greet her. As she put her phone on silence she noticed the incoming text.

Okay - if you think this is what you need to do. I won't stay mad for too long. ;) I love you.

Gigi smiled. She knew that Douglas would come around, and she felt much better going into the meeting with his blessing. She still wouldn't make any decisions, though, without discussing it further with him. She owed him that.

Gigi tried to quiet her thoughts and focus on her conversation with Anna, who was leading her into her office.

"Gigi, it's been a long time since we've seen you here," Anna said. "I must admit that I was a bit surprised to see your meeting in my calendar."

"Yes, it has been a long time. And thank you for working me into your schedule."

"You know, we were all so sad to hear about the tragic loss of the Sinclairs—and then the daughter. God, that must have been so awful for you. I can't even imagine."

Gigi was nodding her head. The agency had sent beautiful flower arrangements for both memorial services, and Anna herself had called Gigi with her condolences.

"Yes, it really was the most awful time of my life—particularly losing Ari." Gigi's eyes filled with tears thinking about it, as was often the case no matter how much time had passed. "But you know. It's true what they say about it getting easier. And Douglas has helped me with all of that."

"Yes, we were all very pleased when we saw your wedding announcement in the papers. We agreed among the office that you two seemed the perfect fit for one another. Douglas sure does seem to be taking to marriage well." Anna laughed.

Douglas and Anna knew each other from various social events, and he was the known bachelor among her and her friends. Gigi had known this when she and Douglas started seeing one another. At first it had felt awkward to her—back in the early days of the courtship, when she'd attended various events with him. But Anna and her friends were among the crowd that made it easier for her, being very accepting and inclusive.

"Thank you. That means a lot to me." Gigi smiled.

"So what brings you in here today? I assume that you are looking for someone? Is everything going okay with Nathalie?"

"No, actually I came here to talk to you about possible positions for myself."

Anna looked genuinely surprised as she sat up a bit straighter in her chair. "For you? Really, Gigi?"

"I know it probably sounds weird. I don't need to tell you that it's not about the money. I'm just looking for something to fill some of my time. And I do miss taking care of a family, if I'm being honest. As strange as that probably sounds." Gigi laughed, trying to make her situation sound a little less serious than what it had become. She didn't need to fill Anna in on all of the details or the frustrations between her and Douglas. She trusted her—but still, it was a small social circle, and she didn't need it to get out there that she and Douglas were having any kind of marriage problems.

Anna looked at her intently for a moment before she got busy on the computer in front of her. "Okay, let's see what I have available right now. I'll just pull some of the listings. Do you have any specifics of what you are looking for?"

"I think ideally it would be something part-time; probably with weekends off would be best."

She wanted to be sure that she could at least allocate long weekends with Douglas in case they wanted to go out of town. Even as she had the thought, her stomach lurched. Long weekends were not going to be enough for any of the travel that they'd talked about doing. No matter how much she tried to convince herself otherwise, Douglas was right about the fact that her having a job was going to interfere with any travel plans that might want to make.

"Okay." Anna was peering at her computer screen. "I do have one job right now. It's in Pacific Heights and they are looking for someone to come in around thirty hours per week. The times are negotiable and they said that the person could have weekends off if they were willing to work the occasional weekend dinner party. Does this sound interesting to you? Gigi?"

Gigi's thoughts had turned back to Douglas and the argument that they'd had the other day about her working again.

"Sorry, Anna. Yes, that might be interesting to me." She knew that her face was belying the interest she was trying to show—that she didn't really feel about the position.

Anna seemed to be studying her for a minute before she spoke. "Tell you what. Why don't you go home and think about this a bit more? If it feels like a fit to you, give me a call back and we'll set up an interview. How does that sound?"

Gigi felt relieved, although she couldn't quite put her finger on it. Thank God she didn't really have to fake her excitement about positions she was less than crazy about these days—gone were the times that she needed the income to survive. She just needed to be true to her own feelings about it. And she knew after being there, after talking to Anna, that getting a job was not the answer. She knew that it felt all wrong to her when she really considered it.

"That sounds good, Anna. Thank you. I'll make a decision and call you within a day or two." She didn't want Anna to feel that she'd totally wasted her time, so she would think about it a bit more; but in her heart she knew that it wasn't what she wanted.

Gigi said her goodbyes at the office and headed to her car, anxious to send a text off to Douglas that she was on her way home. Suddenly she wanted nothing more than to curl up in his arms and hear about his day.

On my way home, honey. I've decided it's a no to a job. I'll stop bothering you about that. ;) I'm cooking your favorite for dinner. Can't wait to see you. Love you.

She waited a few minutes before starting the car and didn't have to wait longer than that for his reply.

That's good news, love. I can't wait to see you. Love you too, beautiful.

Gigi smiled as she pulled out of the parking lot to head towards home. They were going to be okay. She and Douglas. That she was sure of.

CHAPTER 5

Gigi dished Douglas up a second helping of his favorite pasta dish and refilled his wine glass as she listened to him talk about his day. Most often, she loved the normal times like this at the end of the day. No matter how bad or strange she'd been feeling, she was sure that her life was better for having Douglas in it. She loved taking care of him, spending these quiet moments with him, no matter how else she might be feeling on a particular day. Her life might have started to seem a bit boring to her, but it wasn't her husband that she was bored with. That she was sure of.

"Thank you, honey. Dinner is delicious, as always." He was grinning at her, teasing her in a way, because they both knew that more often than not the meals were take-out. But Gigi had learned to cook a few dishes and Douglas had seemed to enjoy them, so she was determined to expand her horizons in the kitchen.

A cooking class. Maybe that was something she should look into. She mentally put it on her to-do list of things to check out.

"You're so welcome. You are easy to please. Thank God."

They both laughed at her comment.

"So tell me about your day, love—about what happened at the agency."

Gigi guessed that he'd been holding back from questioning her about it since she returned home, but they needed to have the conversation; they needed to put some closure on the issue of her getting a job.

"Well, first of all, I had a great chat with Lia finally today. We've been playing phone tag a lot lately, so it was nice to connect with her."

"How are she and Antonio doing? Did she invite you to come stay with her?" Douglas winked because he knew that the two of them were always planning a next visit together, something that Gigi knew that he would always encourage—especially now, she thought.

"They're doing great and she sends her love. Yes, we did talk briefly about a visit soon. Would you like to go? I told her that I thought you might like to spend some time with Antonio at the vineyard. I know it's something that interests you, yes?"

Douglas was nodding his head. "Yes, we can go there whenever you like. I'm up for anything, and if you think its something you want to do, I can call the travel agency tomorrow."

"Well, I told her that I was going to hold off for just a bit." Gigi looked down at her plate, feeling slightly ashamed to tell Douglas her reasons for wanting to wait.

"Really? What's wrong, Gigi?"

She was trying to hold back her tears, but it couldn't be helped. Her emotions were all over the place these days and she couldn't hold them back now.

"Oh, I don't know. And I told Lia as much. I did share with her how I've been feeling. This feeling in the pit of my stomach about what it is I'm supposed to be doing—how I've been feeling so confused lately about this stage of my life." She looked up at him and saw the hurt in his eyes. "It's not you, honey. I promise you that. And I'm sorry to put you through this. I know it's not been easy for you lately—that I've not been easy lately."

Douglas reached across the table to grab her hand. "Darling, you don't need to apologize to me for anything. I only want you to be happy. Really. I wish that I could make you happier—that I knew what to do to help you fix whatever it is that you're feeling. And I do understand—about the job. If it's what you want—what you need—I'll be fine with that. I promise."

"You know, while I was at the agency, talking to Anna, I decided that it wasn't what I really wanted after all. She did have a part-time job to tell me about but as she was telling me about the position, it just didn't feel right to me. And I think that you have a good point about that type of commitment interfering with our travels, with our time together."

Douglas was nodding his head and seemed to be

listening intently to her as she expressed her thoughts about it.

"I don't want anything to interfere with the time that I have with you. I worked too hard to finally get you to stop working, to let you have a moment of regret about doing so." Gigi laughed but there was certainly a hint of truth to the statement, as they both knew how difficult it had been for Douglas to cut down on his work as a lawyer.

"Honey, just in case you ever doubt it, I have no regrets about leaving my job to spend more time with you. You're the best thing to happen to me in a long time." He brought her hand up to his lips, a gesture that Gigi never tired of.

"Well, then I think we are on the same page, in that whatever we figure out for me to do around here, it's not going to be something that keeps us from spending more time together."

"Agreed." He smiled widely. "Now, back to your meeting with Anna. We'll be seeing her at the charity event next week. You have that on your calendar, yes?"

"I do, yes. In fact, that's one reason that Blu and everyone are coming this weekend. She's been working on a dress for me." Gigi winked.

"Now that I can't wait to see."

Douglas never tired of Gigi's buying new things for herself, and he was always very generous with his compliments to her, no matter what she was wearing.

Being married to Douglas was the best thing she could have done for her self-esteem. Douglas made her feel young and beautiful all the time. And she knew how lucky she was to be married to such a romantic man.

"Oh, speaking of the charity event—there's something I wanted to show you." Douglas crossed the room to his briefcase, returned, and placed a magazine in front of Gigi on the table.

Gigi read the headline out loud. "A Story of Hope in Guatemala."

"It's actually the second time this week that the organization has come to my attention. Greg—you know, my golfing buddy?" Gigi nodded. "His grandson joined us the other day. Their class is collecting money for the orphanage. I told him that I wanted to find out a little more about it, but that we'd get back to him. Then just today I saw this article."

Gigi and Douglas had become very involved in numerous charities and organizations. They knew that between the two of them—with Douglas's very large nest egg and investments from his career as a lawyer, and the enormous inheritance that Gigi had been given by Arianna—they had more than enough money to live lavishly the rest of their lives. But that wasn't to say that they just threw their money at things without thought. Gigi really appreciated that about Douglas, and it was something that he had taught her—because being able to give so generously was a rather foreign thing for Gigi, who had worked hard all of her life just to be able to support herself.

Gigi had quickly skimmed the article and was now folding the page over to show it to Douglas. "Oh, Douglas. Their little faces." She felt the tears forming in her eyes for having read about the lives of so many of these children and then seeing picture upon picture of their big brown eyes filled with hope—smiles on their faces, seemingly oblivious of the fact that anything was wrong in their world. Well, of course one couldn't tell that from an article and a few pictures, but she thought that they looked happy despite their rough start in life.

"I know. The pictures got to me too, I must say. And Matt, Greg's grandson, had a lot more material with more pictures of the kids and the place where they are living. What do you think? Shall I write him a check and send it over tomorrow?"

"Hmm."

"What's hmm, darling?"

"Did you read this whole article? The part about their huge volunteer department and what all of their needs are? This is quite a thing they are doing. And the part about the American couple. It's very interesting. Very commendable, I'd say—to give up so much of their lives for these kids."

"Yes. It's an incredible story. Do you agree with me then? About a donation?"

"Oh yes, a hundred times yes. I can't think of

anything right now that I'd rather see our money go to."

And Gigi felt the hint of something stirring within her. It wasn't something she'd be able to put into words just then, but somehow the pictures of those children had touched her, and looking at Douglas across from her now with the checkbook he'd retrieved from his briefcase— she knew that it had touched him too.

PAULA KAY

CHAPTER 6

Gigi sucked in her stomach, trying to be discreet about it while at the same time barely containing her laughter.

"Gigi, stop." Blu laughed as she attempted to put pins in the appropriate spots of Gigi's new gown without sticking her. "You don't need to do that. Your figure is gorgeous."

"Oh, you are way too kind."

"No, I'm serious, and you know that I fit a lot of women. You've done a great job keeping yourself in shape. You should be proud. And I know how much Douglas appreciates your curves." Blu winked.

"Well, Douglas is very good for my ego. This is true." Gigi laughed. "I really love the dress, by the way. You've outdone yourself, and you must let me treat you to something while you're here."

"Don't be silly. I love designing for you, and just getting away for a few days is treat enough for me—for all of us. Chase has been working a lot of hours lately and I've been pretty busy with the new line—and the girls, of course."

They both looked over at eighteen-month-old Kylie, who seemed to be sleeping peacefully in the playpen that Gigi had set up for her in the corner of the room.

"She really is so gorgeous, Blu. I'm guessing that Chase is as happy with fatherhood as you seem to be with the newest addition to your family."

"Ya know, he really is a great dad. I knew that he would be." Blu smiled widely, and Gigi was reminded of everything that she'd seen the young girl go through since she'd known her.

She'd liked Blu since the first day Arianna had brought her and her daughter Jemma to the house for dinner. Arianna had been just nineteen then and it was a rough time between her and her parents. Mr. and Mrs. Sinclair hadn't really approved of any of Arianna's friends and Gigi had sensed their quick judgment of Blu, with her punky hair, tattoos, and young daughter.

But Gigi had a different sense about the girl. A sense that had been right on as she saw the intense love and loyalty for Arianna that would come to pass over the years ahead. Blu was there for Arianna like no one else had been, and Gigi would always be extremely grateful for that.

Blu was nudging her playfully. "Penny for your thoughts."

"Oh, sorry. What were you saying?"

"I was just mentioning how excited Jemma had been

when she found out we were coming up. She really does adore you and Douglas. Even though I know she can be a bit of a pain sometimes."

"Well, I haven't noticed anything out of the ordinary so far. She's always pretty polite to us; but I have seen her throw some serious attitude your way, so I think I have an idea what you are talking about. I guess maybe it's her age?"

Jemma had just turned eleven, which Gigi could hardly believe. She'd known the young girl since she was three and definitely seen her go through some significant changes in her life. In her opinion, it was bound to be challenging for the child—going from a life in San Francisco, where Blu had worked three jobs to earn a decent living for them, to the beach house in La Jolla, where Blu had developed her very successful career as one of America's finest clothing designers. Gigi knew that Jemma now had more of the things that wealth brought, but it also meant sharing the attention of Blu.

"Yes, I'm sure it does have to do with her age—this whole pre-teen period I keep hearing about." Blu's words interrupted Gigi's own thoughts about the child. "And I have been keeping an eye on her—ya know, to see how she's doing with all of the changes. First there was the adjustment of having my mom move in with us, then before you knew it she had a new sister to share the limelight with, and after all that, the wedding. I suppose it's a lot for a child to deal with, really."

Blu and Chase had gotten married just six months ago. He'd moved in well before that—before Kylie was born—but Gigi was sure that all of it did mean a lot of changes for Jemma.

"She sure seems fine to me. Happy as ever with Chase, and I've seen how sweet she is with her sister."

"She really is, and I'm grateful for that—especially grateful to my mom. It's been so helpful having her with us through all of the transitions. I had no idea how challenging the home schooling would be, and I honestly don't think I'd have been able to do it without her. But she's a natural at teaching. I will say that." Blu smiled as she talked about her mother.

It was so wonderful for Gigi to see how much their relationship had grown over the past few years. It had been a bumpy road, but one that had seemed to be playing out amazingly well when all was said and done.

"I do hope that you told Linda that she was invited this weekend. She's always welcome here any time."

"I did, yes. And thank you. She does know that and really enjoys her visits with you two. We'd made the decision together that it would be a nice break for her to stay home this weekend. She doesn't really get that much time to herself these days, so I thought it might be nice for her. I even surprised her with a little spa day package, which I really hope she'll take the time to enjoy."

"Well, that does sound lovely."

"We've got a busy month coming up. Mom and I will

head to London with the girls for a big fashion show and some meetings I have scheduled. Chase will join us later, and I've booked us all into a place in the south of France for a few weeks. You and Douglas should join us. Sorry, I've been meaning to ask you about it. There's plenty of room, and I think it will be very nice and relaxing. I know how busy you both are these days." Blu winked and Gigi got the joke, as she'd told her on more than one occasion that she'd been feeling a little bored.

"Thanks for the invite. I'll run it past Douglas, but I feel like Europe may be a few months away for us. I was also talking to Lia about a possible visit. Are you going there too?"

"Yes, I think we'll probably fly to Italy before we come back. It seems a shame not to, and I know that she's dying to see Kylie again. So—"

"Mom!" Jemma burst into the room, interrupting the conversation. "Chase and Douglas are not being good sports."

"Jemma, that's pretty rude, you know. You just interrupted our conversation—and you might come in to say hello first."

"Sorry, Mom. Hi, Gigi." She took a step to put her arms around Gigi's waist.

"What's the problem, honey?" Gigi asked.

"Well, Chase and Douglas beat me at the game we were playing, and I don't think it was fair at all because they've had a lot more practice than what I've had."

"What game is that?" Gigi asked, knowing before doing so that Douglas had gotten the horseshoes out, a game that he never tired of playing with his buddies over a few beers.

"The horseshoe game—and I suck!"

"Jemma Lynne! Watch your mouth!" Blu scolded her loudly and then went to pick up Kylie, who was stirring in her playpen.

"Sorry." Jemma looked from Blu to Gigi. "I'm bored. What can I do, Gigi? Will you take me shopping?"

"We're not here to go shopping." Blu was shaking her head and giving Gigi a look which Gigi took to mean that it was in reference to their earlier conversation about Jemma's behavior issues.

"But Mom, you said that you would buy me a new outfit. I haven't gotten anything new all week."

Gigi was shaking her head, wondering at what point Jemma had started acting so spoiled. She hated the thought and she did love the child dearly, but it was not a nice display of attitude at all. Blu really does have her hands full with her if she doesn't get on top of that. And as quickly as she had the thought, for some reason her mind turned towards the orphanage that she'd read about. Jemma needed to visit a place like that—needed to see how nice she really had it and that not all children were as lucky as she had been. But she didn't say any of these things out loud. It was none of her business—not until Blu asked for her advice, anyways.

Gigi turned to Jemma before Blu could reprimand her again for her attitude. She knew the child was very close to being sent to her room. "Jemma, how about if you play with Kylie for a few minutes so that your mom and I can finish up here. Then I was hoping that you would bake some cookies with me. I have a new recipe to try that's full of all kinds of sweet ingredients."

Jemma nodded her head, smiled, and went across the room to take her sister from her mother's arms, seemingly content in the moment to let the adults finish their fitting.

"Sorry about that. See what I mean?" Blu said to Gigi under her breath.

Gigi nodded. "She'll be okay. Just don't let it get any worse." She laughed, trying to make light of it.

PAULA KAY

CHAPTER 7

Gigi and Blu were quiet for a few moments, each lost in her own thoughts as Blu worked to finish her adjustments to the dress. Finally, when Gigi noticed that Jemma was playing with Kylie out of earshot, she turned to Blu to speak about what was on her mind.

"Do you ever think that all of the money we have is a bad thing? I mean, I know it's different for you—because it's not just the inheritance but also your success as a designer—but for me, I don't know. Sometimes it still feels odd."

Blu looked up at her as she placed one last pin along the hem of Gigi's dress. "You can step down now. I'm finished. Let's sit here for a few minutes, as long as Jemma and Kylie seem content."

The two women crossed the room to sit at the small table by the window, and Gigi waited for Blu to express her thoughts.

"Do I think the money in itself is a bad thing? No, I don't. But I think I do know what you mean. I think it has changed things for me and Jemma. I'd be blind not to admit that it's changed her—that I've let that happen, I mean. It's weird because even when I see myself doing it—spoiling her—I know that it's not good. But it's hard to not want to give her all of the things that I never could before. Things that I never had myself, growing up. Does that make sense?"

Gigi looked at Blu carefully before she spoke. "I do understand it. Yes. But I also think that Jemma is going to have some problems—or maybe not problems exactly, but she is acting a bit spoiled for sure, if I'm being honest."

"You can always be honest with me." Blu smiled, grasping her friend's hand in her own. "I know that you only want the best for Jemma. You've always just wanted the best for both of us. And I appreciate that so much."

"Well, I suppose that Jemma is not really much different from Ari when she was her age. I mean, I loved that child, but she would have been called spoiled by anyone." Gigi laughed, thinking of the tantrums that the young Arianna used to have when she didn't get something that she wanted. Yes, she had turned out okay—in the end. But then again, how would she have been without the accident—without her own illness and being faced with her death. She'd been forced to look at her life differently, to realize that many more things had mattered to her than the material wealth she'd grown up with.

"Yes, you do have a point about Ari. God, my first

impression of her was that she was a pretentious snob. Definitely not someone who would want anything to do with someone like me." Blu laughed. "I'm sure that we were quite the odd pair of friends to others."

Gigi smiled. "Ari loved you so much, Blu." Her voice was quiet and sure. "You were one of the best things to happen to her, and you came into her life at just the right time—who knows the path she might have gone down had she kept hanging out with all of her friends back then who only wanted to party? But she became just a bit more serious about her life once she met you."

Blu laughed in response. "Well, she still had her days, for sure. That girl could party with the best of them." Blu's voice got quieter too as the memories came. "But I know what you mean. We were a good team, she and I."

The two women were quiet for a moment, and Gigi guessed that Blu was being flooded with memories of Arianna, just as she herself was.

Blu looked at her intently. "So back to you, though—and what you were saying about the money. Do you think it's been a bad thing for you?"

Gigi thought about the question being directed back to her. "No, I wouldn't say it's bad necessarily. And I know that even without the house and the money that Ari left me, Douglas and I would live a very good life. He's worked hard for all of the savings that he's accumulated for retirement. And it's not that I don't appreciate everything. I do." Gigi sighed.

"But?"

"Oh, I don't know. I sound foolish and a bit ungrateful even talking about it."

"Gigi, no one would ever accuse you of being ungrateful. That's not who you are."

"I guess I'm just feeling a little unsettled. I'm not feeling content, if that makes sense. Sure, I'm happy with Douglas and the time that we now have to spend together, but I'm not so sure there's a lot of meaning in my life besides that; and I guess it's making me feel a bit depressed lately, if I'm being honest."

Blu frowned and Gigi felt the need to put her friend's mind at ease.

"Oh, I shouldn't have used the word depressed, I guess. It's not as bad as all that. I promise."

Blu nodded and seemed to accept her explanation as Gigi continued.

"I just feel a bit empty. Like there's something missing. I thought that maybe getting a part-time job—with another family—might help, but I've come to the conclusion that it's not what I'm looking for either."

"What does Douglas think about everything?" Blu asked.

"Oh, the poor man. He's probably at his wit's end with me, honestly. But other than the odd argument now and again, he's just trying really hard to please me—to help me find the thing that's going to make a difference."

"Hmm."

"What's hmm? I'm open to any thoughts and suggestions." Gigi smiled at Blu, encouraging her to voice her opinion.

"Have you thought about volunteering or something? Or maybe getting more active with one of the charities that you and Douglas support?

"It's funny you should mention that, actually. Let me go get something to show you."

Gigi returned after a few seconds with the magazine article that Douglas had shown her a few days earlier. "I can't get the faces of these kids out of my mind."

Blu skimmed the article and Gigi waited for her response.

"I can see why. What an amazing thing this couple has done." Blu was looking at Gigi intently. "What are you thinking? It does say that they take volunteers."

"Oh, no. I wasn't thinking about that, really, at all. I mean, maybe if it was just me; but I don't think that Douglas would ever go for it. Heck, in reality I'm sure that I'm too old to be doing something like that. But—"

"But what? And no, you are certainly not too old. Not by a long shot," Blu said.

"But I just can't stop thinking about it, I guess—the kids, I mean. It's really done something to me for some reason."

"It's that motherly instinct in you." Blu smiled wide. "That doesn't surprise me in the least."

Gigi nodded. She supposed that was it. The feeling

that she'd been having to want to scoop those kids up in her arms.

"Well, we can definitely donate to the organization, and we will do that. Douglas is making some phone calls to find out exactly what their needs are."

"Maybe there is something that you can spearhead here—in the U.S.—to help raise money and awareness for it. That seems like just the type of project that could cure this sense of boredom you've been having, my dear." Blu winked.

"That is actually a great idea. Maybe you're right about that." Gigi reached over to pull Blu in for a hug. "Oh I'm so glad that you're here. I feel better already for having talked to you."

"Any time, my friend. And I'm glad we're here too. I've missed you."

CHAPTER 8

Gigi found herself missing the chatter of Jemma beside her while she cleared the dinner dishes from the table. It had been a great weekend, and the house now felt so quiet with just her and Douglas alone again. She'd invited Blu to stay on longer, but they had the upcoming London trip to prepare for, so the weekend visit had been a quick one. They'd gotten the fitting for Gigi's dress done, and Blu had promised to ship it to her within a few days so that she'd have it in time for the event later that week.

"Honey, come here for a sec. Quick." Douglas was calling out to her from the family room where he'd disappeared for a drink and some television after dinner.

"What is it? Are you okay?" Gigi's heart had lurched for a moment as she rushed into the living room to find Douglas engrossed in something on the TV.

"Sorry. I'm okay. I want you to see this." He pointed toward the TV screen. "They're doing a special news segment on volunteering and look at what it's featuring."

Gigi looked up at the screen and when she did, she saw little faces similar to those of the article about the orphanage in Guatemala. "Place of Hope," she read out loud what was being displayed across the bottom of the screen. "Is that the same orphanage as the one in the article?"

"Yes, can you believe it? Honey, I think the universe is trying to tell us something about this orphanage." He winked at Gigi and pulled her by the hand to sit down in his lap as they finished watching the segment together.

Gigi's heart was racing. She thought the universe was trying to tell her something, alright. It was the kids. She couldn't stop thinking about them.

"That is quite the coincidence, isn't it?" she said to Douglas after the program had ended. "What do you think we should do, honey?" She was curious as to what his thoughts were about the whole thing.

"I think I should make some phone calls tomorrow. I want to call Greg's grandson first and talk to him about a donation, and maybe he knows of someone that he can put me in touch with—to see what their real needs are, I mean. I'd like to make a significant donation—if that's okay with you, darling."

Gigi was nodding her head. "Yes, of course. I think we should, too—"

"Okay, spill it. But what? I can see it in your face, hon." He was teasing her, and she loved that look on his face.

"Well." She glanced at him to see that she had his full attention. "What about what they were talking about on the news show?"

He looked at her with a question in his eyes. "What's that?"

"The volunteer part of the program." Gigi was almost afraid to bring it up—she hadn't really thought about it much until now, but after her chat with Blu and then the TV program, something about it felt oddly right. "I mean, who even knows if they'd accept us? We're probably too old." She laughed before Douglas had a chance to respond. "I'd actually said as much to Blu earlier when we were talking about it."

"You were talking about the orphanage with Blu?"

"Yes. Well, to be honest, she'd asked how I was doing and we were talking about ideas for getting me out of this li'l funk I've been in." Gigi leaned over and kissed Douglas on the cheek before continuing. "So I showed her the article about the orphanage. We were mostly talking about donations and maybe starting a fundraising project for it—you know, as a way for me to focus on something positive."

"As a way for you to stop feeling so bored with your retirement—and your old man?" Douglas winked, but Gigi wanted to be sure that there wasn't hurt beneath his words.

"Oh, honey. I promise you that it has nothing to do with you. You make me insanely happy. I mean that." She squeezed his hand and kissed him on the lips.

"Hey, I think the fundraising project is a great idea. I can ask about it when I make some phone calls tomorrow, if you like."

Gigi was nodding her head. "Okay. That would be good." She looked Douglas in the eye.

"And?"

"And does that mean that you are totally opposed to the idea of volunteering?" She felt a bit foolish even asking. Even in her mind, she could think of a list of reasons why it was a bad idea.

"Oh, honey. I really don't think that would be a good idea for us. I mean, traveling in Guatemala would not be anything like travel in Europe. I think it would be hard for us.

"I know. I'm sure you're right. It was just a crazy idea after seeing it on TV." Gigi tried to hide the disappointment that she was feeling. She tried to talk herself into feeling something other than what her heart had been telling her.

"Let's see how I make out after my call tomorrow. I'm sure we can find a way to be involved from here. I promise you. We'll find a good compromise, okay, honey?"

He kissed her then and Gigi laid her head back against his chest, willing the faces of the children to leave her mind for the rest of the evening.

Gigi tried to focus on the gossip Evelyn was telling her. They hadn't had coffee in ages and she really did want to catch up with her friend, whom she hadn't seen for so long. She'd known Evelyn for as long as she'd worked for the Sinclairs. They'd shared many a gossip session back in the day—about which housekeeper was about to lose her job, whose boss was having an affair, and any number of day-to-day things that only "the help" tended to know about. But today she just couldn't focus. Or maybe she really didn't care all that much anymore.

"So, what's wrong with you?" Evelyn said, breaking into the scattered thoughts that Gigi was having. "You don't seem like yourself and you've hardly said two words the whole time we've been here."

Gigi thought for a minute before answering her friend. She knew that there was a division now between her old friends and her new life. She didn't want it to be the case, but she'd started feeling it shortly after Arianna had passed away and even more so once she'd married Douglas. She was no longer one of them.

She had tried at first—to keep in touch and get together just as she'd done when she was working, but several of her friends stopped returning her calls and making excuses whenever she'd attempt to get together— at least that's how it felt to Gigi. Evelyn wasn't like that, though. The two of them had known one another the longest, and Gigi counted her as a genuine friend.

"Oh, I just haven't been myself lately, I guess," Gigi

said after several seconds had passed.

"How so?"

"It's hard to explain, really. And I know it probably sounds silly. I just feel—I have this sense of unhappiness. I don't really know how to explain it except to say that I feel pretty bored half the time."

Evelyn raised an eyebrow, and Gigi started to feel slightly annoyed at herself for mentioning it.

"I went into the agency the other day."

"Really?"

Evelyn was definitely surprised by this statement.

"Yes, I was thinking that maybe a part-time job might be good for me for a while. Take my mind off things and, you know—have someone to take care of again."

"Gigi. You do have Douglas to take care of. And sorry to say it, but do you know how many people would kill to be in your shoes?"

"Yes, I know. I don't mean to sound ungrateful. And I'm not. I'm just trying to figure some things out, I suppose. Forget I mentioned it." But she knew that she couldn't take it back.

Evelyn got up from the table to come around and give her a little hug. "Don't be like that, Gi. That's not what I meant. You know you can still share stuff with me. And of course I want you to be happy. It's just that it's kind of hard to hear you talk like that when so many good things have happened to you."

Gigi felt her mouth go tight as she looked to her

friend to continue.

"Oh, I don't mean what happened to the Sinclairs—or to Arianna—God rest their souls. Of course I don't mean that. But everything else. Everything good that you do deserve. You know?" Evelyn said.

"I know. I do. And of course I've thought about what you're saying too. I'm lucky to have Douglas—I know I am. I'll be fine."

Gigi stood up to give Evelyn a hug goodbye, anxious now to be heading home.

Douglas had texted her earlier to see what time she'd be home, and she had yet to respond to him. She sent him a quick text now before she started her car to head towards the house, her thoughts on the conversation that she'd had with Evelyn and how ridiculous that she feared she'd sounded.

PAULA KAY

CHAPTER 9

Gigi came in the front door, anxious to have a chat with Douglas about his day. He'd left right after a quick breakfast, and she'd not spoken to him, which wasn't typical of them. She smiled as she realized how much she did miss him, even when it was only a day that went by when they saw each other less than normal.

She called out a greeting, noticing that her favorite classical music was playing and the house was quite dark.

"Hello, my love." Douglas was by her side quickly, kissing her on the cheek and taking her by the hand towards the living room.

The room was lit by a big fire he had going in the fireplace and the various candles placed around the room.

"Douglas, what's all this?" She noticed her favorite takeout Italian meal set up on the nice china on a blanket in front of the fireplace. The conversation she'd just had with Evelyn flashed in her mind. She was so lucky to have Douglas—he really was romantic and thoughtful. "Did I forget an anniversary or something?" Gigi laughed, allowing Douglas to pull her down next to him on the sofa.

He smiled at her before taking her face in her hands and kissing her gently. "I just really wanted to do something nice for you—to surprise you."

Gigi stared into his eyes intently before returning his kiss with one of her own. "You surprise me every day, darling—by how wonderful you are to me." And she meant it. She knew that any unhappiness that she was feeling didn't matter. Douglas would make everything okay. Being loved by her husband would make everything okay.

Douglas reached over to the table in front of them to hand her the champagne that he'd already poured. "Darling, I have a surprise for you."

She loved the look that she saw on his face—the glimmer in his eye as if he was about to share the most marvelous of secrets with her.

She took the glass from him and waited as he picked up his own. "Well, honey, I've already said yes and we've sealed that whole marriage deal a few years ago." She laughed, curious as to what was going on.

"Funny that you should bring up our marriage." His eyes shone. "That's a perfect tie-in to what I have for you tonight."

"Is it?" Gigi was playing along, enjoying the banter between them.

"Do you remember my vows to you? The part where I told you that loving you had opened my heart up to adventure again?"

Gigi's eyes instantly filled with tears. She remembered their wedding day in the garden as if it were yesterday. "Yes. I remember. You promised that our every day together was going to be a new adventure." She leaned over to kiss him softly on the lips. "And it has been, Douglas. Every day."

Douglas looked her in the eyes for a moment before he pulled away to reach behind and get something from the sofa. He held up his glass of champagne for her to reach out her own for a toast.

"Here's to our next adventure, darling." He grinned widely as he placed something on Gigi's lap for her to see.

Gigi looked down and back up at him in shock when she saw the two tickets to Guatemala lying in her lap. She didn't attempt to stop her tears as the reality of what he'd done hit her. She was almost afraid to put the question into words.

"The orphanage? Really, honey?"

Douglas wiped her tears with his hands, before he held her face gently. "Really. Your happiness means everything to me."

They kissed again and Gigi felt more content than she'd felt in months. An adventure indeed. She was ready for it.

PAULA KAY

CHAPTER 10

Douglas squeezed Gigi's hand from the backseat of the car as they weaved in and out of the airport traffic coming from the airport in Guatemala City. Gigi was feeling tired after their eight-hour flight, but any fatigue she felt was being overcome by excitement over their arrival.

"Wow, we are certainly not in Kansas any more," Douglas joked as they both peered out the windows.

Gigi laughed. "No, we are not." She squeezed his hand. "And I love it."

She'd not felt this alive for a long time. Douglas had been right on with surprising her with the trip, and she loved him dearly for knowing her so well—for knowing what she needed and being willing to give that to her, even though she knew that it wasn't really his idea of something fun to do in their retirement. But he'd assured her several times that if it made her happy, he was fully on board. He'd go anywhere in the world with her to see her content and smiling. And she believed him—that he loved her that much. She leaned over now to give him a kiss.

"What's that for, my love?" He smiled at her sitting beside him.

"Oh, I just love you so much. And I want you to know how happy you've made me."

He laughed. "Well, we'll see how happy we both are a few weeks from now. Or which one of us is missing our comforts of home the most."

Douglas had done a lot of research prior to their departure date, filling Gigi in on some of the precautions and risks of being in a less-developed country—a place where they did have to be smart about safety issues and also the various health concerns. But he'd lined everything up for them—visits to the clinic to get the proper shots and pills, informing himself about the area of the country where they would be staying, and everything else that he could do to help them to feel as prepared as possible.

"Is this your first time here to Guatemala?" the driver asked them.

Frank and Loretta, the founders of the orphanage, had hired a car and driver to greet them at the airport, making that transition quite smooth for them upon their arrival.

"Yes, it is," Douglas said. "And so far, it looks quite hectic out there." He laughed as he referred to what seemed to be some crazy driving outside of his window.

The driver laughed. "Oh, this is is nothing. You

should see it during the busy time. But soon we will be out of the city. You will notice a difference on the roads."

"How far is it to the orphanage—to Antigua?" Gigi asked.

"Not too far. Once we get through this traffic, we will be there in about thirty or forty minutes." The driver smiled as he glanced at them in the rearview mirror. "You will like Antigua. Many of the tourists like it the most, I think."

"We're very anxious to see it," Douglas said.

"And the rest of your country," Gigi added.

"Your English is very good," Douglas said to the driver.

"Thank you very much. I spent two years in America—I have a brother there—in Florida. Hablas español?"

"No, not really," Douglas said. "But maybe we will learn a little bit while we are here."

"There are many good language schools in Antigua. Maybe I can recommend one for you?"

"I think we'll be pretty busy at the orphanage, but if that changes maybe we can contact you."

Gigi knew that Douglas was only being polite—that he didn't really see the need for learning Spanish, as they'd only be there for a limited time, and Loretta and Frank had assured him that they'd get by just fine with their very limited knowledge of the language.

When Douglas had told her that he'd signed them up

for a month with the volunteer program at the orphanage, Gigi had agreed that it seemed like more than enough time. Secretly though, she thought that she might like to be at the orphanage for a bit longer, but she knew better than to press her luck on the subject. Douglas was being such a good sport about it all, and he did agree that they'd stay on as long as they liked in order to travel a bit and see some of the country. The fact that he was willing to do that much really did surprise Gigi. They were both used to traveling in quite a luxurious way, so to say that they'd be a bit out of their element here would be an understatement.

After they'd gone for several miles, Gigi squeezed Douglas's hand as she looked out the window at what she guessed was Antigua. "It's so lovely, isn't it?"

Douglas nodded his head, seeming also to be caught up with the view out his window.

There were colorful buildings and what Gigi thought must be a volcano off in the distance. She'd read about them and had an ambition to hike one of the volcanoes after they were finished volunteering at the orphanage.

She and Douglas had laughed about how thankful they were that they'd put their regular exercise routine into place months before, per their doctor's recommendation for their general good health. They had been comfortably doing many of the gorgeous hikes that were available to them in Marin Country where they lived. They were both feeling very fit, which Gigi felt quite proud of at her age. So some hiking in Guatemala seemed like a very doable thing to Gigi, and would only enhance this grand adventure that they were on.

Gigi's thoughts were interrupted by the driver, who was pointing out a lively outdoor area to them.

"You can come here to buy many local items and sample some of the good street food of Antigua."

Gigi was fascinated by the women she saw out the window. There was a large square with a grassy area and benches in the center, and local women selling various items throughout. They were dressed in vibrant-colored clothing, and Gigi found herself looking forward to a time when she and Douglas could come back to check out what all the items were that they were selling.

"Honey, can we come back to this part of town soon?" Gigi directed the question to Douglas, but it was the driver who spoke up.

"The orphanage is not far from here. You can easily walk during the day or take a taxi at night if you'd rather not walk during the dark."

"Is it safe? To walk around here at night?" Douglas asked the driver.

"Yes, you should be fine. Just mind your wallet and purse. The biggest issues in this part of the country would be petty crime such as that, not as much any violent crime to worry about here."

"As we'd do back home in the city—using our common sense, I mean," Gigi said to Douglas. "I don't feel too worried about safety here. Do you, honey?"

"No, not really. But we'll just take care to know where we are going."

"Many of the volunteers and staff of the orphanage come to the main part of town a lot. I'm sure someone will be able to show you all of the best restaurants and coffee shops around town. The volunteers seem to need their burgers and beers." The driver laughed and Gigi thought she detected a hint of something in his voice.

"Well, I for one will be wanting to sample some of the local food before we go for any burgers. Do you feel the same, honey?" Gigi said.

"Yes, I agree." Douglas looked at her. "And I suppose after we're here for a few weeks, a burger or some other western food will have a certain appeal to it, won't it?"

Gigi nodded her head in agreement, already thinking about corn tortillas with rice and beans.

The two were silent in the backseat of the car, each lost in their own thoughts as they watched the new scenery out the windows.

"We are almost to the orphanage now. This is the street where you will be staying," the driver said.

"This looks almost like it could be any neighborhood in the states," Gigi said.

"It does look much more—I don't know—residential, maybe? Than what I'd imagined it would be," Douglas said.

"Here we are." The driver had pulled the car into a big carport at the side of what looked like a very large house.

Gigi could see the sign placed above the front door; she read it out loud. "Place of Hope." She leaned over to give Douglas a quick kiss. "Looks like we made it. I can't believe that we're here."

She could hardly put into words the excitement she was feeling. Something about being there—pulling up in front of the actual orphanage—was making her heart pound wildly in her chest. She looked over at Douglas as he was making his way around the car to open her door.

"Wow, it is really hot here," he said as Gigi got out of the car.

She laughed as the full force of the heat struck her outside the air-conditioned car. "Yes, I suppose we'll want to change into more suitable clothing right away."

They hung back for a minute as the driver carried their luggage onto the front patio of the house. After a few seconds, Douglas brought Gigi's hand up for a kiss.

"This is it, my love. Our big adventure is about to begin. Are you ready?" He winked at her and Gigi giggled.

"As ready as I'll ever be." She pulled him to her for a kiss on the lips, not bothering to wipe the few tears away that were on her cheeks. "Thank you, Douglas."

CHAPTER 11

Before Gigi and Douglas had made it to the front door of the house, a woman with dark curly hair popped her head out with instructions to the driver about the luggage. Gigi recognized her right away from the article and segment they'd seen on TV. It was Loretta, the American founder of the orphanage.

"Gigi, Douglas." The woman extended her hand for them to shake. "It's so good to meet both of you. I'm Loretta." She turned towards the man standing beside her. "And this is my husband Frank."

Frank stepped out to shake their hands. "How was your flight?"

"A little long, but the flight itself was good," Douglas said.

"We're very excited to be here—to have a look around," Gigi said, smiling. "So far, what we've seen during the drive has been pretty interesting."

"Yes, you'll have some time for exploring tomorrow."

Gigi noticed Loretta giving Frank a look before she continued.

"We'd love to show you around the orphanage, and then we have reservations for a nice dinner scheduled," Loretta continued.

"I'm actually surprised that I don't hear any children." Gigi laughed lightly but in truth she thought it was very odd that the house was so quiet at this time of the afternoon.

"Oh, the kids are doing their studies right now. We have them on a pretty strict schedule—it's what we think is best for them." Loretta took the hand that Frank was offering her as he stepped in to continue what Gigi couldn't help but feel was a rehearsed conversation.

"We try to run the orphanage somewhat as a boarding school, with a focus on their studies and coming away from here with the ability to get jobs—"

"Or to continue with their studies." Loretta interrupted.

"What about the smaller kids? It seems like we saw several on the TV program we watched that were not school age?" Douglas asked.

And Gigi knew that he was asking on her behalf. All of the kids had touched her of course, but it was the little ones in particular—the ones that hadn't had a chance yet to know as much love or heartache—that Gigi felt drawn to. And she had shared as much with Douglas.

Gigi couldn't be sure but she thought she saw another quick glance pass between Loretta and Frank before Frank responded to Douglas's question—glances that were making her just a bit uneasy, if she was being honest with herself.

"Well, we sometimes partner with another child care organization in town that takes care of the younger children. That's part of the footage that you probably saw on that TV segment," Frank said.

Douglas was nodding, and Gigi could tell by the look on his face that he was deep in thought. She guessed that something about this initial conversation was not sitting right with him either.

"So, how exactly do you partner with them? We're looking forward to seeing more about how the orphanage is run here and what your day-to-day operation needs are," Douglas said, directing his question again towards Frank.

"You know, we'll be able to answer a lot of your questions later—during the tour and over dinner. I'm guessing that you two might like to freshen up and maybe have a little rest before we show you around a little bit?" Loretta said.

Gigi nodded. "And hopefully we can meet some of the kids?"

"Yes, although we might save that for tomorrow. We don't like to get the kids too riled up before bed, and they'll be excited to meet new people from America," Loretta said, smiling.

"Many of the children dream of being adopted by Americans—or of moving to America to go to college once they finish their studies, so they are always very interested when our American volunteers arrive," Frank said.

Gigi nodded her head in agreement, but she felt quite disappointed to learn that she might not even be seeing the children until the next day. She was anxious to connect with them—it was what she was most excited about—and the plans that Loretta and Frank were laying out for the evening seemed rather boring to her. She'd rather stay and eat dinner with the kids, in truth, but she held her tongue, not wanting to appear rude. Besides, they would be here for a whole month. There would be plenty of time for playing and helping with the children. At least she hoped that it would be the plan for them while they were there.

"Let me show you where you will be staying," Loretta said, motioning for them to follow her into the house for the first time.

Gigi looked up at the beautiful chandelier she saw as she entered the enormous foyer. The area was really quite spectacular. There was a table with a huge bouquet of flowers and a wide staircase on either side of the room. If she didn't know better, she could have been entering any home back in her own neighborhood of Sausalito. It was so unlike what she'd expected the orphanage to look like that she couldn't help feeling shocked.

Loretta seemed to notice her look and Gigi tried to put on a neutral smile.

"Wow. It's really beautiful," Gigi finally managed.

"Thanks. We like to surround the kids with the kind of living environment that we try really hard to get them adopted into—the steps lead to where the children sleep," Loretta said. "We'll be able to show you around upstairs tomorrow."

Gigi noticed Douglas's furrowed brow. Something was bothering him and she didn't imagine that he was going to be silent about it much longer.

"What exactly do you mean by the kind of living environment?" he finally managed, directing his question towards Loretta. "Do you mean that they are only adopted by wealthier people, people that can afford to live in homes with expensive chandeliers?"

Gigi cringed. Douglas's sarcasm was apparent, and he'd raised the question that was bothering her also. She thought Loretta looked a bit taken aback—maybe at a loss for words as she seemed to be looking to Frank to help her out.

"Well, yes. The reality is that many of our clients—potential parents—are very wealthy. It is a difficult process to adopt a child from this country and it does require a fairly large investment. It's unfortunate, but there's a lot of red tape involved here. Do we have kids being adopted by people, other than the very wealthy? Sure we do, but to be honest, it's not who we target with our campaigning—"

"And we don't apologize about coming from the

same social circles ourselves," Loretta interrupted her husband.

Gigi definitely detected a note of defiance in her voice, and she couldn't help but worry that she and Douglas were now totally getting off on the wrong foot with their hosts. This initial meeting was not going very well. She sighed, looking at Douglas. But it was also what she appreciated about him—his willingness to speak his mind and ask hard questions to get at the truth of the matter. She knew that there'd be a big conversation coming between them just as soon as they were alone together.

Loretta was forging ahead with her speech, mostly directing it at Douglas, who was clenching Gigi's hand more tightly by the minute.

"It's what has allowed us to find good families for many of these children—being able to use the influence that we do have back home—we won't apologize for that, because it's giving these kids a chance that they never would have had without us. We're proud of what we do here." Loretta reached over to hold Frank's hand as she finished speaking, looking more than a little frustrated.

Gigi touched Loretta's arm lightly. "I don't think Douglas meant to upset you. We believe that the work you are doing here is quite amazing. Isn't that right, dear?" she directed to Douglas.

"Yes, yes. I'm sorry if I've upset you. Please don't take my questions the wrong way."

Loretta was nodding her head and smiling now.

"It's just my nature to want to fully understand what it is that my wife and I are supporting. And we do want to support you. We wouldn't be here if that wasn't the case," Douglas said.

Gigi admired her husband's effort to try to get things back on track between them and their hosts. She really couldn't wait to talk to him when they were on their own. She was dying to hear his real thoughts—his first impressions of everything—to see if they matched her own.

"No worries." Frank was reaching out to shake Douglas's hand, his other arm around his wife's waist. "Loretta just gets a little passionate about the work we do here—it's been a big investment of time and money for us, so I'm sure you can understand where we're coming from."

Douglas nodded.

"Absolutely. So let's just leave it at that for right now and, like you said, there will be time for more questions later—questions that I'm sure we'll have." Douglas laughed and the two men started walking down the long hallway, Loretta and Gigi following close behind.

They followed Frank as he took them past a huge dining area with multiple big tables and elaborate place settings already set up. From the large windows, Gigi could see a big courtyard outside, bordered on three sides by the home. She imagined that this might be where the children played, but other than the basketball hoop and the tennis court she could see in the distance, it didn't seem all that inviting to kids, in terms of a play area. She wondered again what the children were doing. It seemed to her that they'd be having a little playtime after a day of school, but they were nowhere to be seen.

After several seconds and a few hallways, they arrived at what seemed to be a separate wing of the house.

"This is where you will be staying," Loretta said, opening the door wide for them to enter their guest quarters. "We've put you in one of the private suites. Down the hallway are several other shared rooms where the volunteers sleep. You'll be meeting them soon."

Gigi stepped into the big room, again feeling like she could have been entering a quaint little B&B back home in Marin County. "Wow, it's really beautiful." She walked further inside, taking in the large seating area, huge bed, and what looked to be a spacious bathroom off to the other side. The decor was impeccable. She could tell that no expense had been spared in making the room as "Americanized" as possible. Again, she was feeling shocked at how different it was from what she'd expected, but she was definitely going to hold her tongue until Loretta and Frank had left them alone. She glanced over at Douglas, hoping that she could catch his eye and somehow relay to him that he should also mind his words.

"Everything looks lovely," Douglas was saying to

Loretta. "I'm sure we'll be quite comfortable."

"Great. We'll let you two rest a bit. How about if I come by here to get you at six o'clock? We have a reservation for a restaurant at seven-thirty. So that should give us time to give you a tour and then head over for dinner," Loretta said.

Gigi looked at her watch and saw that they'd have two hours. The idea of a short nap was suddenly very appealing to her.

"That sounds perfect. Thanks for everything," Gigi said.

"We'll look forward to dinner," Douglas said.

And then Gigi and Douglas were finally alone.

PAULA KAY

CHAPTER 12

Gigi crossed the room to sit next to Douglas, who'd already taken a seat on the large sofa in their room. He grabbed her hand and pulled her closer to him.

"How are you feeling, darling? Tired?" He asked.

Gigi closed her eyes for a second, which made her realize just how tired she really was. "Yes, I suppose I would like a little nap before dinner." She put her hand on his knee as she looked up at him. "What about you? Are you tired?"

"Not so much tired as I am confused and just a tad annoyed still."

Gigi sighed. "I know what you mean. I couldn't wait until we were alone to talk." She let Douglas take her feet into his lap while she laid her head down on the opposite side of the sofa, appreciating how good it felt to finally lie down for a minute. "What are you thinking, honey?"

"Well, what are you thinking?"

Gigi studied his face for a second before she responded. She was trying hard not to jump to conclusions—to remain open about everything until they had more information, until they'd spent more time with Loretta and Frank and, more importantly, the children.

"I have to admit that my first impression of the place—of them—is nothing like what I'd anticipated." Douglas was nodding his head in agreement. "They just don't seem—the place doesn't seem like the same orphanage we saw on the news program, does it?"

"No, it doesn't. Not by a long shot, actually. It's what's been bothering me the most, along with the statement Frank made about campaigning. I mean, I do get it, but it's a strange word to use in relation to the needs of the kids here, don't you think?" Douglas was looking at her intently, waiting for her response.

"Yes, I agree. The whole thing was odd. I feel like the segment that aired on TV was potentially only a half-truth about the situation here. In the program—and really in the magazine article too—they certainly portray themselves as having a facility that cares for children of all ages, including the little ones, who it's now pretty obvious to me do not actually live here."

"Yes. We're going to have to get to the bottom of all this. As uncomfortable as it all might be, we need to know what we're investing in—who we're investing in and what their genuine motives are," Douglas said carefully.

"I agree. I still don't want to jump to any conclusions yet. We haven't seen the kids or spoken to any of the other volunteers. Let's try to keep an open mind about it.

Don't you think? For a while, I mean—while we do the actual work that we came here to do," Gigi said, really hoping that they could be on the same page with it all, because she didn't want their experience to end before it had even started.

"Of course, darling. I agree, and I think we'll have a much better idea over the next few days as we see the day-to-day operations of the place." He seemed to be studying her face again before pulling her up to kiss him. "Don't worry, love. I'm sure everything is going to be fine."

Gigi nodded and tried to stifle a yawn behind her hand.

"Now why don't you crawl into bed and have a little rest? I'm going to stay up and do some reading, so shall I wake you in an hour?"

Gigi kissed him again. "That sounds like a lovely idea. Thank you."

Gigi sat opposite Douglas in the seating area of their room after a nap and shower, feeling refreshed and more positive. She noticed that Douglas seemed to be studying her, with a funny smile on his face.

"What's that look?" She flashed him a smile, waiting for a teasing comment that usually promised to please her.

"Oh, nothing. Just enjoying how lovely you look. And happy," Douglas said.

"I am happy. Regardless of what happens here, I'm going to appreciate the experience. I've already made my mind up about that."

"Good. Me too." Douglas smiled. "And don't worry. We will find you some babies to hold." He laughed but her heart jumped when he said it. She was determined to get to the kids—regardless of what Loretta's ideas were of what they should be doing while they were here.

Before long, Loretta was knocking on the door and they were heading out to finish the tour of the building and grounds—everything except actually seeing the kids, which Loretta had promised they would be doing first thing in the morning.

"And what time do the kids eat dinner?" Gigi asked as they passed by the dining room. "I would have thought maybe we'd get a glimpse of them eating tonight before we go out."

Loretta looked at her watch. "Oh, they eat pretty early—at five o'clock—so that they can be doing their homework in their rooms by six, which is where they are now."

Gigi nodded, holding her tongue. They certainly did seem to have a focus on studies around there. Not that it was a bad thing, just that from what she'd heard so far, they didn't seem to be giving the kids any free time—for playing or just hanging out.

The thought reminded her of when Arianna was

young. After seeing the young girl go through a very rough few months with a packed schedule, Gigi had finally had a much-needed talk with Mr. and Mrs. Sinclair about how overtired she was. In her opinion, it had just been way too much—piano lessons, tennis lessons, horse-riding lessons, various clubs at school, the private tutor, plus all of the social invitations that Arianna was getting to various birthday parties and such.

She had feared being so vocal about her thoughts, but in the end the schedule did change and the Sinclairs seemed to respect her for voicing her strong opinion. They had trusted her by this time and knew how deep her love for Arianna was, Gigi practically having raised the little girl since they'd adopted her as a baby.

"And this is where the children practice their various instruments."

Gigi was jolted out of her memories as Loretta gave them a tour of yet another wing of the spacious building. There was a large room with a baby grand piano and several smaller rooms leading down a hallway where the kids could practice any number of different instruments.

"We have a few local music teachers come in a couple times a week to give the children their lessons. Each child must pick at least one instrument to master throughout their time here—"

"We believe it's a good discipline for them to learn." Frank interrupted his wife as he entered the room, greeting Gigi and Douglas for the first time since they'd parted ways a few hours before.

"Oh, good. You made it." Loretta turned to Gigi and Douglas. "Frank had a meeting with a couple of potential donors who are in town."

"Never a quiet moment." Frank laughed.

Gigi caught Douglas's eye as they followed Loretta and Frank out to the car waiting for them in the driveway.

CHAPTER 13

The ride to the restaurant was a short one. Gigi held Douglas's hand in the backseat of the sedan, with Loretta sitting to the left of her and Frank up front with the driver. They made small talk about the weather, and Gigi was reminded of her hunger as her stomach rumbled from a long afternoon without any food. She assumed that they were being taken to have a meal that would feature the local cuisine, and she was really looking forward to trying it.

A few moments later they pulled up to a restaurant that could only be described as something that had been plucked straight off the streets of Rome or any big tourist town in Italy.

"Oh." Gigi couldn't help the surprise from escaping her mouth. "Are we eating at an Italian restaurant?"

"Oh yes, it's one of the best in town. We're actually part owners," Loretta said as they were making their way out of the car. "Do you like Italian food?"

Gigi didn't even try to hide the glance she sent in

Douglas's direction. The annoyance she was feeling was almost laughable at this point.

"I love Italian. It's probably my favorite type of food."

Loretta's smile widened.

"And we had it the night before we flew here." Gigi laughed. "I just assumed that you'd be taking us to a restaurant that is more typical of Guatemala. I've been reading up about it and am quite anxious to try the local cuisine."

"Oh, I don't think you'd be missing much not to eat it." Loretta laughed. "We'll be sure that you get a taste. It's mostly corn and beans, with lots of chilis thrown in. Personally, I prefer the restaurants that offer international menus when I go out, but we do offer a mixture in the dining room back home."

Gigi was trying very hard to hide her irritation, but quite frankly Loretta was really starting to grate on her nerves. Was Loretta really thinking it so odd that Gigi and Douglas would come all the way to Guatemala with anything less than an expectation of eating some local food? Douglas reached for her hand and leaned in to give her a quick kiss as they were walking into the restaurant.

"It's okay, honey." He whispered into her ear. "I'll take you somewhere for tamales tomorrow."

Gigi smiled in response, squeezing Douglas's hand. He had spent several nights prior to their departure, patiently listening to Gigi recount her daily research about

the country that she was so excited to visit. He'd heard
her talk about all of the various types of tamales and how
much she couldn't wait to sample the different varieties.
She sighed as they made their way to one of the best
tables in the room. There'd be plenty of time for her and
Douglas to eat exactly what they wanted. She'd try not to
let her frustration ruin the evening. Besides, she was
starving by this time and pasta did actually sound pretty
amazing.

Frank ordered a bottle of wine for the table and then
excused himself to go talk to the chef.

Loretta said, "We've just hired a new chef from Italy.
It's all been very exciting the past few weeks, as the
restaurant has been getting good reviews so far. We have
a goal for it to get some great exposure through some of
the top food and travel blogs, so Frank's been quite busy
here lately."

"You two certainly do seem to have your hands full."

Loretta nodded, acknowledging Douglas's comment,
and Gigi guessed that she was totally oblivious to the
undercurrent of sarcasm. She was beginning to wonder if
Loretta and Frank were even interested in the children of
Guatemala at all. Try as she might to keep her initial bad
impressions at bay, everything that Loretta and Frank
seemed to do or say appeared to be focused only on
business. Gigi wasn't naïve, in that she knew running an
orphanage had to be a lot of work—a lot of which was
about business—but she was finding the lack of emotion,

or even discussion about the children, to be very off-putting and just overall strange. She reached for Douglas's hand under the table as Frank returned to take his seat and lift his glass of wine for a toast.

"To our new friends, Gigi and Douglas. Here's to what I hope will be a long relationship to come."

They all raised their glasses as Gigi added, "And to the children—who I can't wait to meet."

Douglas squeezed her hand and leaned over to give her a kiss on the cheek.

"Yes—to the children," Frank said as he and Loretta clinked glasses with Gigi.

"I hope you don't mind, but I've taken the liberty of ordering up some of our favorite pasta dishes and a few appetizers. We've got some new items for the menu that I've been anxious to try; they promise to be very delicious," Frank said.

"No, that sounds wonderful. I'm suddenly realizing just how hungry I am after our travel day." Douglas laughed. "I'm pretty sure that I could eat just about anything right now, but your menu looks very nice."

"I'm sure that you two are quite familiar with great Italian restaurants, and good food in general—coming from the Bay Area and all," Loretta said. "Frank and I have been to San Francisco a few times and we've always really enjoyed trying out new restaurants there. In fact, the chef that we have at the orphanage was hired from there."

"Really?"

Gigi saw the look on Douglas's face that matched the surprise that she was once again feeling about something that had come out of Loretta's mouth. She saw Loretta nodding her head, and waited for Douglas to continue.

"I would have thought that you'd be hiring local people to help you at the orphanage?" Douglas didn't miss a beat as he continued.

"Well, it's not that we don't hire any locals at all," Frank said.

Gigi thought that finally Frank was looking just slightly uncomfortable—as if he felt the need to have to justify some of what was coming to light.

"We hire local people for the cleaning and also for the Spanish portion of the children's schooling."

"And for the music lessons." Loretta interrupted her husband, obviously feeling the need to get that bit of information in there again.

"Yes, as we said earlier, our main goal is to get the kids adopted and in order to do that, we try very hard to get them acclimated to what their new lifestyle will be— most probably in the U.S. or some other western country."

"And we do have a very high success rate," Loretta interjected.

Gigi could sense Douglas fidgeting beside her without having to look at him. She knew that he was about to be very angry, and she really hoped that they could keep the conversation going without coming to harsh words. If she knew one thing about her husband, it was that he rarely held back his thoughts when he felt that something was wrong. And this conversation—their whole initial interaction with Loretta and Frank since they'd met them earlier in the day—was not going well at all. Something was most definitely amiss.

"Surely the couples who are adopting these children don't want them totally removed from their culture—their heritage. That's not what you're suggesting, is it? Because it sounds like you're saying that you want them to go to the U.S., or whatever privileged country they end up going to, and just lose their whole past identity—their sense of what it means to be Guatemalan."

Gigi could see the red surfacing on Douglas's neck. She wanted to try to diffuse the heated conversation, but at this point she knew that she was just as invested in hearing the answers to Douglas's questions as he was.

"We're not suggesting that the kids should lose their identity. We just know how hard the transition can be for them. We've found it to be best if they're more prepared to deal with it. It helps them to adjust better—feel less homesick once they are away," Frank said.

"And since many of these kids are older, teaching them English is one of the best things that we can do for them here. To place them in an American elementary school or junior high school without knowing the language puts them at a huge disadvantage, as you can imagine. Sure, they can start with an ESL program—"

Loretta stopped when she seemed to notice the question on Gigi's face. "English as a Second Language—most of the areas where our kids end up living have these programs available in the public school systems."

"But the faster they can mainstream into regular classes, the better for them and their opportunities to be accepted in their new schools." Frank continued from where his wife left off.

Gigi squeezed Douglas's hand underneath the table. "Okay, I do understand the need for teaching the kids English. That all makes perfect sense. I think maybe Douglas is a little surprised about the fact that an American was hired to cook for the kids—rather than finding a local chef, I mean." She looked to Douglas as she spoke and he nodded his agreement. "And—well, just all the focus there seems to be on 'Americanizing' the children, for lack of a better term—that's kind of what it seems, from what you've told us."

"Our sous chef is Guatemalan," Loretta said, appearing anxious to clarify that point to her guests. "So when I mentioned about the kids getting local food as well as international, they do have that option every day also."

"Oh, that does seem nice," Gigi said, thinking that maybe she needed to cut them a break again—wondering if Douglas was feeling as forgiving with his own thoughts about the couple and all of the conversation that had taken place so far.

"Oh, that looks delicious," Douglas said, as two waitresses started placing heaping plates of pasta and various appetizers down on the table in front of them.

Gigi felt relieved for the diversion that their food promised, and silently vowed to speak about friendlier topics for the remainder of dinner. Maybe she and Douglas just needed a good night's sleep and a fresh look at everything in the morning. And the kids. Tomorrow they'd be able to spend some time with the children, which was all that she really cared about anyways.

"We do it family style here, so please do help yourselves to whatever you like." Frank motioned to the dishes in front of them as Douglas served himself and Gigi a piece of bruschetta that Gigi thought looked amazing.

"Bon appetit," Loretta said.

Gigi let her mind go clear of earlier thoughts while she enjoyed the feast in front of her, thankful that the conversation during dinner seemed to be turning towards less heated topics. They'd figure everything out soon enough. She trusted that she and Douglas could get to the bottom of it in terms of how they felt about the orphanage and the organization—more so about Loretta and Frank, really, as that was so far the basis for any misgivings that they might have. For now, she'd enjoy the rest of the dinner and look forward to finally seeing the kids in the morning. Somehow she felt that that would go a long ways towards any negative thoughts that she might have about being there.

CHAPTER 14

Gigi stirred in bed, trying not to wake Douglas beside her as she reached for her phone to see what time it was. She felt his arm come around her, pulling her towards him.

"Come here, woman."

She sighed as she felt his kiss on her neck.

"What time is it, love? It feels very early to me."

"It's only six thirty. But do you smell that breakfast?" Gigi laughed. "I can't believe that I'm saying this after all the pasta we had last night, but I'm famished." She turned herself so that she could see Douglas's face. "Do you want to join me?"

He seemed to be thinking about it for a moment right before he pulled the comforter closer to his face.

"I think I'll try to catch just a few more minutes in this comfy bed, if you don't mind."

Gigi nodded, leaning down to kiss him quickly on the cheek. "I don't mind at all. You rest up. I'm counting on a busy day for us."

Thinking about the day ahead brought back some of

that initial excitement that she'd felt yesterday as they were first arriving. She was determined to go forward with a fresh perspective—they both had decided that after returning from dinner last night. They'd get a good night's rest and then try their best to put the earlier conversations and misgivings aside, so that they could view the operations of the orphanage and see the kids with an unbiased viewpoint.

Douglas seemed to be studying her as she got ready.

"What are you looking at?" She smiled.

"You and how lovely you are."

"You're too kind to me." She laughed and came to sit by him on the edge of the bed before making her way to the door.

"I bet you're excited to see the children, aren't you?"

Gigi nodded. She couldn't wait to finally see the kids. It was all she could think about since she'd woken up. "I doubt the kids will be up this early, though."

"Oh, you never know." Douglas laughed. "They seem to run a pretty tight ship around here, and that just might include breakfast at the crack of dawn."

"Honey." Gigi tried to look stern.

"I know, I know. I do have an open mind. I promise." He pulled her to him for one last kiss. "You go see what you can find and I'll come join you in a little while."

Gigi found her way to the dining room, mostly due to

the strong smell of eggs and bacon, rather than her
memory of how to get around the large building. She still
couldn't quite get over how spacious the home felt to her.
As quickly as she had the thought, she was willing it out
of her mind. Keep an open mind so that you can really
have fresh eyes today.

She stepped into the large dining hall and nearly
gasped out loud in her surprise at seeing it full. She
guessed that there were about forty kids eating quietly at
the large tables. Just as she was scanning the room,
looking for Loretta or Frank, she saw a young woman
making her way towards her with a big smile on her face.

"You must be Gigi." The woman extended her hand.
"I'm Sarah, the person who is currently in charge of
organizing the volunteers."

Gigi shook her hand and returned the warm smile
with one of her own. "It's great to meet you. My husband
and I are excited to learn more about what we'll be doing
while we're here."

"Oh yes, I thought we could have a little meeting
after breakfast if that works for you. I'm sorry that I
wasn't here to greet you yesterday. One of the volunteers
was celebrating a birthday, so we had quite a party at one
of the bigger clubs in town." She laughed as she gestured
towards a half-full table. "Which is also why several of the
volunteers are still in bed."

"Oh? Is that an issue?" Gigi cringed inwardly as the
words left her mouth. She might need to bite her tongue a

bit, as she suspected by the makeup of the group she saw now at the table that she and Douglas were going to be the elders of the bunch.

"Oh, no. No issue." Sarah laughed and didn't seem bothered by Gigi's comment. "Honestly, there's not that much to be done around here right now, and we have way more volunteers than are needed. We're actually splitting shifts as it is, with plenty of days off for sightseeing for those who prefer it."

Once again Gigi felt shocked by what she was hearing. How could everything be so different than what she'd imagined it would be—from how it had been portrayed on the TV segment and in the magazine article? What she and Douglas had read and watched was an outcry for help—a plea to provide time and money for the orphaned children of the area, many of whom had been babies and toddlers, their tear-stained faces luring her from the moment she'd first laid eyes on them.

She couldn't help but feel that someone had clearly not done their proper research—or they'd been duped by the people running the place—the people, meaning Loretta and Frank. She sighed. Her idea of giving them a second chance wasn't going to be as easy as she thought—at least not from the looks of things already that morning.

"Sorry, what was that?"

She'd been so lost in her own thoughts that she'd completely missed what Sarah had been telling her as she pointed across the room.

"I was just saying, why don't you go help yourself to the buffet and come join us over here. I'll introduce you to the early gang this morning anyways and you'll meet the others a little later."

Gigi nodded and made her way to get some breakfast. She hoped that Douglas would be along shortly, as she suddenly felt the need for some reinforcement for how she was feeling.

As if reading her mind, she saw him entering the dining room as she was making her way back to the table where the volunteers were sitting. His eyes lit up when he saw her.

"Oh, good. I see that I'm just in time. And look at all the kids." He laughed. "You must have been pleasantly surprised when you saw that the room was full."

Gigi nodded. "Can you believe how quiet they are, though? I still don't quite know what to make of it. I'm about to sit down over there with the volunteers. Get some breakfast and come join me?" She gave him a quick kiss before he headed for the buffet and she made her way back to Sarah and the other volunteers.

Sarah made quick introductions for Gigi and then again a few minutes later when Douglas arrived back at the table.

"So are you both feeling rested or are you still tired from your travels yesterday?" Sarah directed to Douglas.

"No, no. We're pretty rested, I think. I know that

Gigi is dying to dig into some work today. We're both anxious to see what's in store for us while we're here."

"And we're very ready to work." Gigi chimed in. "I especially can't wait to spend some time with the children. What will they do after breakfast?"

Sarah looked towards two of the volunteers. "Shane and Lisa are in charge this morning of making sure that the kids get ready for school. So they'll go upstairs to brush their teeth and collect their books. School will start at seven thirty, so there's not a lot of time, really."

Taking the cue to get up, Shane and Lisa excused themselves to go get the children moving from breakfast.

"Wow. School starts early, doesn't it?" Gigi said.

"It does, I suppose, but the kids don't seem to mind their schedules. They really do quite well here. And it give us—the volunteers—plenty of time to do other things."

"Like?" Douglas said.

"Well, the main other thing that I have them doing right now is stuffing envelopes with information for potential donors. And whatever other types of related things that Loretta needs us to do."

Gigi felt her heart pounding faster even before she asked the question that was on her mind.

"And what about the other organization—the one with the younger kids that need more care?"

She thought that Sarah looked confused by her question, and she felt her heart sinking.

"Loretta told us that the smaller kids—all of the

footage and photos that we'd seen on the news show—
were with another organization here in town that they
also work with."

Sarah was nodding her head but still looked a bit
confused. "I think I might know what group you're
referring to. I guess we'll have to ask Loretta about that.
I've not been made aware of anything that they are doing
regularly with them—at least not in the month that I've
been here."

Gigi felt her shoulders slump.

"But we'll ask Loretta about it, okay?" Sarah seemed
to sense Gigi's frustration at the lack of answers she was
getting.

Gigi nodded, feeling disappointed again.

PAULA KAY

CHAPTER 15

Gigi and Douglas spent the next few days with Sarah and the rest of the volunteers, mostly stuffing envelopes and doing everything but interacting with the children. At Gigi's insistence, she did spend time with the kids after school while they were doing their homework, and a few times she'd been able to sit in on some classes. But the day-to-day routine was getting to her, if she was being honest with herself. She did understand that the volunteer program had many aspects to it—that there were many things running behind the scenes of an organization—but it wasn't what she'd come for and after discussing it with Douglas, they were getting prepared to have a chat with Loretta and Frank.

With so much free time available to them, she and Douglas had gotten into a routine of taking a mid-morning walk and then going for a coffee at a cool local spot they'd found.

For the first few days, they'd been invited to go to coffee with the other volunteers, most of whom were in their twenties. Gigi and Douglas had sat with them as they talked about their travels and complained about the lack of good beer and pizzas. Many of them seemed to be working at the orphanage as a way to extend their stay in the country, getting free room and board in exchange for the few hours that they were asked to work during the day. Gigi had yet to feel any sort of connection with any of them and wondered again how they could have been so wrong in their expectations.

It wasn't long before they'd searched for an alternative cafe, hoping to meet some local people and interact a bit more with the people living in Antigua. One day they found a delightful little spot, far from the main stretch of popular restaurants and bars, but not too far that they couldn't walk to it. The shop was part cafe and part art gallery, run by an American woman named Jess. She featured artwork by local artists and held regular shows and events to support them, as well as different charitable causes throughout the city.

Today, when Gigi and Douglas walked into the shop, Gigi noticed Jess deep in conversation with another woman at a table in the corner.

"Gigi, Douglas, good morning. I'll be right with you." Jess looked up to greet them, flashing her big smile that Gigi had come to love.

"No worries. Take your time." Douglas said as they seated themselves nearby.

After a few more minutes, Jess walked over to them with the woman that she'd been sitting with.

"Gigi, Douglas, I'd like you to meet Tori."

Gigi thought Tori looked to be in her thirties. She wore a pair of overalls and had her long dark hair pulled back in a loose bun on top of her head.

Tori reached out to greet them with a strong handshake and Gigi instantly liked her.

"Would you like to join us? Please sit down." Douglas stood up to pull the empty chair out for her.

"Thank you." Tori's smile lit up her whole face. "I don't mind if I do."

"Where are you from, Tori?" Douglas asked.

"I'm from the Bay Area, but I've not been back there for several years."

"Really? That's where we're from too," Gigi said.

"How funny. What brings you to Antigua? Are you doing a language course, here on vacation?" Tori asked.

Gigi and Douglas looked at one another and it was Douglas who spoke next. "We're here doing a volunteer program with one of the orphanages."

Jess had arrived with their coffees and Gigi was pretty sure that she saw a quick look pass between the two women at the mention of the orphanage. They'd already spoken to Jess about it when they'd first met her, and they both felt that she'd been holding something back regarding her opinion of Loretta and Frank, whom she did know of.

"Place of Hope?" Tori asked.

"Yes, that's it. Do you know it?" Gigi said.

"Yep, I sure do." Tori laughed.

Gigi saw the question on Douglas's face, and Tori seemed to catch it also as she continued.

"I also volunteered there. Four years ago—when I first arrived."

"I sense a story coming," Douglas said.

"Well, it's not so much a story about my time there. Let's just say that it wasn't for me."

Gigi and Douglas looked at one another and Gigi spoke next.

"We're not sure if it's for us either, honestly." She sighed. "We've been trying to make it work and of course we feel committed to what we signed up for, but—" She looked at Douglas, hoping he'd jump in with something appropriate to say.

"It's just not turning out to be what we thought it would be—mostly in terms of the interaction with the children, which is what Gigi had really been looking forward to the most."

Tori had been nodding her head while Douglas spoke, and Gigi guessed that there was a lot more that could be said about the orphanage, but she was intrigued by this woman and wanted to know more about her time here.

"So, Tori, you said that you'd been away from the Bay Area for years? Have you been traveling all of that time?"

"Oh, no. I've actually been here in Guatemala. Like you two, I came to volunteer with Place of Hope, but now I'm working with a different orphanage—I have been for the past four years or so."

"Really? Is it here in Antigua?" Gigi felt her heart beat faster as she reached for Douglas's hand beside her. She didn't need to say out loud what she was thinking. She knew that he'd be well aware of how exciting this conversation was to her.

"No. It's a place in the jungle—on the river—the Rio Dulce. It's called Casa de los Niños and it's run by a fantastic Guatemalan woman named Silvia."

"The Children's House," Gigi said, grinning at Douglas. "Is that not the best name?"

Douglas winked and squeezed her hand under the table. "Please tell us about this other orphanage."

Tori went on to tell the story of how she'd met another volunteer who took her to Casa de los Niños for the first time—about her meeting with the Guatemalan woman who'd given her entire life to creating a home for the orphaned children of Guatemala. Even as she told the story, the tears were streaming down her face and Gigi felt her own tears threatening to come.

"And, well—as they say, the rest is history. The place—those kids—have had my heart ever since." Tori was wiping her eyes and grinning broadly.

Gigi could hardly speak for all of the emotion she was feeling, but she had to find out more.

"Are you going back?" she finally managed to ask Tori.

"Oh, yes. I'm only in town now to talk to Jess about a

fundraiser that she's doing for the orphanage next month. I'll be leaving to go back Sunday."

Gigi shot Douglas a look, hoping she'd see something on his face that would give her the go-ahead. He smiled, nodding for her to continue.

"Can we go with you? On Sunday?"

Tori grinned, and her look said it all. "Yes, of course you can. I do need to warn you, though—"

Gigi felt her heart drop momentarily. "Oh, does she even want more volunteers right now? I suppose you need to check with her first, which we understand."

Douglas was nodding his agreement.

Tori was laughing. "Oh no. Trust me, we need all the help we can get. There's only Silvia, me, and a handful of other volunteers right now. So, as you can imagine, we have our hands full. It's just that I feel the need to let you know that the accommodations and—well, really everything—it's quite basic. Nothing at all like what you have at Place of Hope." She seemed to be studying them intently, waiting for their reaction.

Gigi said, "I'm sure that I'm okay with all of that. It sounds like what I was expecting before I arrived, so I'd already mentally prepared myself for much less than what we've had so far." She laughed, thinking that for the first time since they'd started working there, she felt excited again.

"And jungle living is not like what you have here. Just laying it all out there. The nearest restaurant is a thirty-minute ride by boat, so we spend most of our time on the grounds with the kids. We have all of our meals together. We do have teachers there right now, but often the volunteers will jump in to help out while the younger kids are napping. So it really is a very big commitment of time."

Gigi felt Douglas's eyes on her and guessed that he had something to say. She didn't want to put him on the spot, but it seemed like some decisions would have to be made rather quickly if they were going to go with Tori in just two days.

"What are you thinking, honey?" Gigi said to him.

"Well, I just think that we need to be careful about our commitment here too—that we at least need to have a conversation with Loretta and Frank before we go heading off to spend time with another organization."

Gigi felt her face fall. Douglas was right, and she knew how he felt about honoring commitments. But they both also knew that they weren't really needed at Place of Hope, not physically anyways, although she guessed that Loretta and Frank were counting on a large donation before they left. Even the thought of it left her feeling bad.

Douglas was quick to interrupt her thoughts. "But yes, darling. I absolutely want to go to check this other place out. It sounds like everything you wanted when we signed up for this little adventure." He laughed and then turned toward Tori as he continued. "Do you think it would be possible for us to come for a few days, maybe a week or so? Or does Silvia require more of a commitment than that."

"As I said, Silvia will just be happy to have you there, period. For as long as you like. I'll phone her tonight to give her a heads-up. Why don't I give you my contact info? You two can have the conversations that you need to have and let me know by tomorrow night if you'll be joining me. How does that sound?"

"Perfect," Gigi said with enthusiasm as they all got up from the table. She followed her gut instinct, being a hugger, and walked around the small table to give Tori a big hug goodbye. "Tori, I can't even tell you how happy I am for having met you today. I feel like this was meant to be."

Tori grinned back at her. "Me too. I'm a big believer in fate myself and my gut hasn't let me down yet. And right now it's telling me that I'm going to be seeing a lot more of you two very soon." She laughed. "But no pressure or anything."

Douglas took the paper from Tori with her contact details on it, and they said a big goodbye and thank you to Jess before leaving the little cafe.

Once alone outside on the sidewalk, Gigi grabbed Douglas's hand and pulled him in for a big kiss. "Oh, honey. Do you have any idea how excited I am right now?"

"I do. Yes." He winked, pulling her to him for

another kiss. "I have a good feeling about this, love."

Gigi had a good feeling about it too.

They made their way hand-in-hand back to the orphanage, Gigi lost in her thoughts about what lay ahead for them, unable to keep the huge grin off her face. The great adventure, phase two, was about to begin!

CHAPTER 16

Gigi looked over at Douglas, who was waiting patiently for her as she got ready for the meeting that they had scheduled with Loretta and Frank. Frank had been away for the past few days, and they'd hardly seen Loretta either once they'd gotten into the swing of things with Sarah and the other volunteers. They were both feeling slightly apprehensive about telling them that they were going to leave for a week to check out Casa de los Niños, but they'd discussed it at length between them and decided that it was best to be honest about it.

When they'd mentioned the orphanage to Sarah earlier in the day, they weren't shocked to learn that she'd heard of it, and they also guessed that there could be a little bit of friction between the two organizations. They suspected that Loretta and Douglas wouldn't be pleased, but they couldn't worry about that too much. They'd already decided that they'd be gone for one week and then come back to work another two weeks at Place of Hope. They were also sure that, no matter what, they'd not leave without giving a donation of some sort to the organization that first captured their interest and their hearts all those months ago.

Place of Hope might not have turned out to be what they'd thought it would be, but they still did see a lot of good happening as a result of the organization and efforts of Loretta and Frank.

Gigi sighed as she made her way over to where Douglas sat reading on the small sofa.

He looked at his watch as she sat down beside him.

"Are you about ready, love?"

Gigi nodded. "I am. I'm just anxious to get this all settled so that we can call Tori and finalize our plans."

"Are you nervous? About talking to Loretta and Frank, I mean?" Douglas said.

"No, I feel confident with our decision. Are you?" She didn't really need to ask him. Douglas rarely wavered once he'd made a decision, especially about something that had caused a certain amount of friction, which had been the case with Loretta and Frank thus far.

"Not in the slightest." Douglas reached into his briefcase beside the sofa and pulled out his checkbook. "I think I am going to write a check today. I'm guessing it might go a long ways with any bad feelings that might come up. Not to say that they won't understand, but just in case."

"Well, we do know that they've been expecting something from us." Gigi looked at Douglas for a few seconds.

"What is it, love?"

"We do feel good about it, don't we? Giving them the donation, I mean?"

"I think so. Yes. As much as I've not agreed with how everything is being portrayed or run, I don't think that there's anything shady going on. Do I think it's much different than how things would be if you and I were running the show around here?" Douglas laughed at the look Gigi sent his way.

"Are you planning on running some things here in Guatemala now, darling?" Gigi winked, enjoying their banter. They certainly did make a very good team—she and her husband.

"No, but you know what I mean. Just in terms of motivation and all."

"I know. Yes, I'd say that they are doing a good thing for these kids, regardless of how they get there. One can hardly argue with the fact that they want them to have good educations and get the best start in life that is possible for them." Gigi agreed. "And leave me to get on with huggin' on some babies now."

Douglas stood up, laughing as he pulled Gigi up to stand beside him. "Well, from what Tori described to us yesterday, it sounds like you'll have more than your share of little ones to cuddle."

"I can't wait." Gigi could hardly stop smiling whenever she thought about what was in store for them.

Douglas leaned in to kiss her. "I can't wait to see you

with them, darling." He took her hand again as he started towards the door. "Let's not keep Loretta and Frank waiting."

An hour or so later, Gigi was humming back in their room as she packed up a small suitcase. Their talk with Loretta and Frank had gone better than she ever would have expected, and the whole thing left her feeling more positive about the couple and their organization than she'd felt since their arrival.

Loretta had said that she understood the draw of Silvia's orphanage and what she was doing in the jungle—that she and Frank had been there themselves and had great admiration for the woman. She stressed that it would be a totally different experience for Gigi and Douglas, in terms of the accommodation and how they'd be living for the next week, but Gigi had assured her that she was ready for something different.

The couple had told Gigi and Douglas that they'd keep their room for them and to go ahead and leave anything behind that they didn't want to take with them. They had even given their blessing in releasing them from their volunteer commitment if they felt that it wasn't what they were looking for. Gigi did notice that this was after Douglas had handed them the sizable check that he'd written for the organization, but she wasn't going to dwell on any bad thoughts now.

She and Douglas were committed to returning, and

they both felt comfortable with the week's commitment in the jungle. Time would tell what would happen after that, and even though she was excited about the differences, Gigi did imagine that it could be an adjustment; she didn't want to pretend that it would all be easy, as much as she liked to think that she was ready for the adventure that jungle living promised.

Douglas had called Tori to let her know that they were all set to make the journey with her the next day. They agreed to meet at Jess's cafe in the morning, and Tori had a minivan coming to pick them up there. The drive to the river could take anywhere from five to six hours and then the orphanage would be another thirty minutes by boat. Tori had sounded very pleased and excited for them when they'd spoken, and Gigi couldn't wait to spend more time with the younger woman. Something about her really drew Gigi in, and she had the feeling that there would end up being a genuine connection there.

From the moment Gigi and Douglas walked into Jess's cafe the next morning, she felt something shift inside her. Jess and Tori looked to be deep in conversation when the couple entered the shop, and Gigi loved the excitement that she could hear in their voices. It was hard to describe, but it was a certain passion that had been evident from the moment she'd first met the two women. It was the passion that she, herself, had been craving in her life.

"Don't let us interrupt you," Douglas called out as he and Gigi picked up the coffees that Jess had waiting for them at the nearby table.

"Oh no. You're not interrupting at all," Tori called out. "Jess and I are just going over some details for the art show next month. Some of the older kids from the orphanage have a few pieces that are going to be featured."

"How lovely," Gigi said.

Tori had shared with them earlier that they'd had a volunteer the year before who was an art teacher. She'd spent hours doing art with the kids and teaching them some skills. Since then, a few of the older children had really blossomed as young artists. Tori and Silvia had been working to get their art featured at a few places around town, starting with the show at Jess's shop.

"Sit, enjoy your coffee." Jess was up from the table and heading behind the counter. "I have some fresh bagels here. You have a bit of a journey ahead, so I figured you might want something to take with you for the trip."

"Thank you. You're too kind to us," Douglas said as he took the bag from Jess.

"We're so thankful for having found this place—for having met both of you," Gigi said, trying to keep her tears from coming. She'd been feeling a little emotional lately, but in a good way—not in a way that had her feeling sad and confused, as was the case prior to leaving for Guatemala.

Somehow she just really believed that they were in the right place—that the timing of everything was perfect and just as it should be.

"It looks like our ride is here," Tori said, interrupting Gigi's thoughts. "Are you two ready?" Tori's grin was wide, and Gigi thought again how lucky they were for having met her.

"I'm ready. Are you, darling?" Douglas said as he got up from the table.

"Yes. I'm so ready," Gigi reached for Douglas's hand.

The three carried their bags out to the minivan and Tori introduced the couple to Juan, their driver, whom Tori said she knew quite well from having taken the trip with him many times before.

Gigi settled back against the seat, ready for the long drive, content to watch out the window and see more of the country. Douglas took her hand and they fell into any easy silence for the first few hours or so of the journey.

Gigi was really enjoying seeing some of the countryside and the little villages that they passed through. She noticed that the people seemed very happy and content. She'd not spent very much time with the local population so far, but when she voiced her thoughts, Juan confirmed that he felt Guatemalans lived a simple, but happy life—content to spend time with their families when they weren't working hard to provide for them.

Juan also timidly asked Gigi and Douglas a few questions about where they came from. He seemed to have a very clear idea of what Americans were like— especially from California, although he didn't express it in a way that was offensive to Gigi. He just seemed genuinely interested. When Douglas pressed him a bit, they found out that most of his opinions came from watching popular American television programs, something that made all three of the Americans in the car cringe.

Tori said, "Although I think that those TV shows are not representative of America as a whole, I can't help but think about the things that I don't miss." She laughed as she looked towards Gigi and Douglas in the seat behind her. "You haven't been gone so long, so I'd be interested to hear your thoughts. Are you homesick at all?"

Gigi looked at Douglas, who squeezed her hand. "It's hard to believe that it's only been about a week, actually. It feels like longer to me. Does it to you, honey?"

"It does. I agree. In some ways, though, it feels like our time is just beginning here now—with this side trip, I mean," Douglas said.

Gigi grinned. "How is that you always seem to be able to read my mind? That's exactly what I was just thinking. I'm not feeling homesick at all. Not yet, anyways. But honestly, we've been living so comfortably at Place of Hope, that I'd hardly noticed much of a change from back home—at least in terms of our accommodation and meals."

Tori laughed. "Well, Gigi, I'm pretty sure all of that is about to change pretty drastically." She looked back at her. "I hope that you're ready for that."

Gigi looked at Douglas and then back at Tori. "Oh, I'm ready."

"I have no doubts actually." Tori reached back to grab Gigi's hand for a second. "I have a strong feeling that you're going to like Casa de los Niños."

Gigi felt the tears coming as she flashed back to the images of the children that she'd first seen in the article and on the television. She had a strong feeling that she was going to like this place too.

PAULA KAY

CHAPTER 17

Gigi could hear the laughter and the shouts of the children before they'd rounded the bend in the river.

Tori looked back at her with a wide grin. "They can hear the boat coming from quite a distance. Wait until you see what's around the corner." She winked and Gigi felt her heart race.

The road trip had gone smoothly, and when they reached the little village where they'd be taking the boat the remaining thirty minutes or so, Gigi thought she'd finally been transported to another world—one that more closely resembled the images she'd had in her head before they'd left San Francisco to come here. This was the Guatemala that she'd pictured.

When Tori had pointed out the few restaurant spots that they could choose from, if and when they did need to get away for a night, Gigi and Douglas had laughed about it. They were only too happy to be away from the western-style restaurants and other comforts that they'd had during their time in Antigua—not to say that they'd probably not appreciate it again by the time they returned.

Gigi was pulled out of her thoughts by the squeals of laughter and the picture that she saw in front of her as the boat rounded the bend in the river.

In the distance, she could see a small wall of children, their brown skin bare and glistening with what Gigi guessed must have been water from the river. She could hear their shouts as they jumped up and in down with obvious excitement and huge grins across their faces.

"Hola, Miss Tori! Hola, amigos!"

Gigi and Douglas laughed as they waved back with shouts of hello.

"Hola, niños. I've missed you all," Tori said as the boat pulled up to the small dock.

Two of the bigger boys reached down to give first Tori a hand, and then Gigi.

"Miss Tori, Miss Tori, Lucía had her baby." One of the little girls came running up to hug Tori and give her the news.

Tori turned to Gigi and Douglas as she hugged the little girl to her. "Lucía is the resident cow." She laughed. "The children have been waiting patiently for the new calf to be born, so it will be pretty big news around here. We've got two cows and a bull here, which is quite a lot compared to what many local people have in the area. As you can imagine, the fresh milk goes a long way."

Douglas was nodding and Gigi quickly felt little wet hands tugging on her. She bent down so that she was eye-level with the small girl whom she guessed to be around five years old. "Hola. You're so pretty."

Douglas bent down too and said, "Bonita" which caused the little girl's face to break into an even bigger grin.

"Si, bonita," Gigi repeated, happy that at least Douglas knew little bits of Spanish. She'd have to practice more while she was here, although Tori had let them know that the children were learning English at school and the volunteers were encouraged to speak English with them as much as possible.

The little girl nearly knocked Gigi down with the big hug that she suddenly delivered. Gigi laughed as she sat down on the pier, pulling the little girl into her lap. "Cómo te llamas?"

She pulled away from hugging Gigi's neck momentarily as she looked up at her. "My name is Jimena." She grinned and for a moment, the name and her expression reminded Gigi of a wide-eyed Jemma from so many years earlier, even though physically the two couldn't have been more different. Jimena was whispering something that Gigi couldn't quite make out.

"What's that, honey?" Gigi asked.

Jimena put her small hands gently on either side of Gigi's face. "What is your name?"

Gigi smiled, her heart tugging already for the little girl. "My name is Gigi. And this is Douglas."

Douglas smiled and sat down beside Gigi as the small circle of children all huddled closer now, each anxious to tell them their names and practice their English.

Gigi could hear Tori laughing just down the dock a bit, a child on each side of her and an older boy carrying her backpack. "Children, let's let Gigi and Douglas get settled soon, okay?"

"Okay, Miss Tori." A small chorus of voices rang out.

"Rafael will come back to help you with your bags and show you where you will be sleeping," Tori called out to them, and the boy carrying her bag turned to give Gigi and Douglas a big grin and a thumbs up.

Gigi and Douglas sat on the dock for a few more minutes, learning the children's names and watching them play. Before long, one child dove into the water, which seemed to demand that they all follow suit, all calling out for the couple's attention as they showed them their swimming skills and various tricks in the water.

Gigi disentangled Jimena's hands from around her neck, where she'd had them for the last several minutes. "Do you want to go back in the water too?"

The little girl shook her head and whispered so quietly that Gigi could barely hear her. "Can I come with you?"

Gigi nodded and quickly brushed away the tears before the child could see them. "Yes, you come with us then."

She was amazed that within a matter of minutes, her heart had fully connected with these kids. It was that silent whisper of something that she'd felt from the moment she'd read the magazine article all those months before. She reached to take the hand that Douglas offered as he pulled her to her feet.

Rafael had returned, and between him and Douglas they carried the two bags that the couple had brought with them for the week. "I will show you to your room now," Rafael said with a big grin, reaching over to tousle Jimena's hair in a way that made the little girl giggle.

Douglas reached out to take Gigi's hand with his free one as they followed Rafael along a path that seemed to disappear straight into the jungle. Gigi squeezed his hand tighter and leaned over to give him a quick kiss on the cheek. "Honey, I can't believe this." She knew that the huge smile on her face said everything that she was feeling.

"You look so happy, love."

"I am happy." Gigi looked down at the little girl by her side. "So happy. I really think this is going be great."

They walked along for only a couple of minutes before finding themselves in a clearing with several worn buildings—well, really Gigi would describe them as several smaller huts with a few bigger buildings that looked in dire need of repair. They continued following Rafael, who led them to one of the smaller huts just a bit away from the others.

"You will sleep here. It is the one with the toilet inside and big bed." Rafael was grinning, and Gigi guessed that he was quite pleased with his English efforts.

"Thank you, Rafael," Douglas said and to Gigi he carefully mouthed the words "toilet inside," looking just a bit confused.

Gigi laughed. She'd already known from Tori that most of the orphanage didn't have modern plumbing—it was something they'd only just been able to implement in a few of the buildings, the others sharing a few different outhouses nearby. Tori had also made sure that Gigi knew about the differences when it came to plumbing in Guatemala—in terms of making sure that any toilet paper was to go into the garbage bin and not directly into the toilet.

It was a big difference to get used to, but Gigi was pretty sure it wouldn't be that big a deal, just as she was confident that they could handle any of the other differences that they might encounter. She made a mental note to let Douglas in on the toilet paper instructions, grinning to herself as she thought about it while she looked around at her new environment. Yes, it certainly was a far cry from Marin County or even where they'd just come from in Antigua. And as she stepped into the doorway of their little hut after Rafael, she couldn't have felt more pleased.

The room was sparse, with only a big mattress on the floor and one small table next to it with a lamp on top and a single wooden chair beside it. She could see where the toilet and small sink were, in the corner of the room just behind a curtain. She caught Douglas's eye as he took the bag from Rafael, thanking him for his help. She imagined that they were probably both having similar thoughts about the comparison with where they'd been staying—and she also guessed that Douglas was as up for it as she was.

Rafael bent down to where Jimena had flopped on the mattress. "Jimena, come with me now, okay? We must let them rest."

The little girl looked over at Gigi. "I will see you at dinner?"

"Si." Gigi scooped her up to give her a hug, and when she set her back on the floor, Rafael took the little girl's hand to lead her out the door.

"Adiós, amigos."

"Adiós. Gracias, Rafael." Douglas shook the boy's hand and the two kids left the hut hand-in-hand, laughing as they ran back down the path towards the river.

Gigi took two steps over to where Douglas was standing, wrapping her arms around his waist. "The kids seem so sweet with one another, don't they?"

"Yes, I was thinking the same thing when Rafael took Jimena's hand just now. They're lovely, aren't they?" Douglas took a small step back to look Gigi in the eyes. "You're lovely—seeing you with them. I think it's possibly the happiest I've ever seen you." He kissed her on the lips and Gigi giggled.

"Well, possibly it's a close second to our wedding day, honey—or the day you asked me to marry you—or the day you first asked me on a date." She grinned at him, feeling everything she loved about their easy relationship.

"Or the day that you finally let me kiss you," Douglas said.

He was teasing her now and all of their talk was bringing with it flashes of Arianna, but Gigi noticed that for the first time in a very long time, she didn't feel only sadness remembering her. In this moment, she was filled with deep gratitude—for everything that Arianna had done for her, but especially for her persistence that she and Douglas were meant for one another. They stood together, embracing, as they both took in their new surroundings for a few moments.

"Do you hear crying?" Gigi asked, tilting her head towards the door.

Before Douglas could respond, there was a quick knock on the door followed by a pleasant-sounding voice calling hello.

Douglas opened the door, and a woman entered carrying a crying baby in one arm and holding the hand of a little girl with the other.

"Hola. Gigi and Douglas, it's so nice to meet you." She disentangled the baby's hand from where she'd been pulling on her hair and handed the crying child to Gigi, all in one motion of stepping inside the room. "Can you try, please? I think she has a bit of a tummy ache. Maria and I have been trying to help her feel better for the last hour, haven't we, darling?" She scooped the toddler up into her arms as she reached her hand out towards Douglas. "I'm Silvia. It's very nice to meet you both. Tori has told me great things about you and I've been looking forward to a nice chat. Do you mind if we sit?"

Without waiting for an answer, Silvia scooted across the bed, settling in with her back against the wall and the little girl nestled in her lap. She patted the bed beside her.

"Come sit. I want to know all about you," she said with the widest grin that Gigi had ever seen.

Gigi and Douglas smiled at one another as they found a spot on the big mattress, the baby now quiet in Gigi's arms.

And it was in that moment that a short, but strong, friendship would begin.

PAULA KAY

CHAPTER 18

Silvia Morales was unlike anyone Gigi had ever met.
The petite forty-five-year-old Guatemalan woman was a
bundle of energy and raw passion—the kind of passion
that was unapologetic and unwavering.

As they talked during their first encounter that day,
Gigi learned that Silvia had been adopted by an American
couple when she was seven years old. She grew up in a
happy home that offered her the privilege of an education
unlike any she could have gotten in her own country. She
was a focused student in the private high school that
she'd attended: that had gotten her accepted by some of
the best colleges in the U.S. She'd graduated from
Harvard and gone on to get her MBA before returning to
her home country with the drive to create a better life for
the children who didn't have the same opportunities that
had been given to her.

"Wow." Gigi looked at the woman sitting next to her,
the young child now napping peacefully in Silvia's lap.
"That's really an amazing story, and your education is
impressive."

Silvia reached out to take Gigi's hand, and the tears in her eyes didn't go unnoticed by Gigi, who felt herself becoming emotional for reasons that she didn't quite understand. "Gigi, I know what you mean—about my story being impressive—but I need to tell you the real reason that I do what I do."

Gigi nodded to encourage her to continue, and she could feel in Douglas's body language that he was being affected by Silvia's words in much the same way that she was. The woman had a certain pure honesty about her that could not go unnoticed. Gigi found herself wanting to know everything about her.

"The children—our home here—is the mission of my life. I believe it's what God created for me to do. From the moment I first got this idea—when I heard that still small voice in my head so many years ago after returning to Guatemala for a visit—I knew that I would spend my life loving these kids—creating a home for them, where they would feel safe and loved."

Gigi felt tears stinging her own eyes as she reached over to give Silvia a hug, nodding to Douglas, who was excusing himself to go for a walk. She smiled as she thought about how sensitive her husband was and guessed that he must have had an idea of the real friendship that was forming between the two women.

It was interesting to hear Silvia talking about God. It wasn't something that Gigi had paid much attention to in her own life—ever since she'd been made to go to Mass as a child growing up in Italy. But looking into Silvia's eyes now, she didn't doubt what this woman believed to be true. Maybe the fact that Douglas and I are here now is a sign from God? She didn't know where the thought had come from but there was no mistaking that feeling inside her—a feeling she'd been having more and more often ever since the day that Douglas had showed her the magazine article about the orphanage.

"Do you know what I mean?"

Silvia's words brought Gigi out of her own head and into the moment again. "I think I do. I'm not sure that most people have such a deep sense of purpose." Gigi wasn't sure why exactly she was crying, but she reached up to brush the tears away. "If I'm being honest, I'm jealous of that."

Silvia looked at her intently. "I think you'll find that soon Gigi. Ask God. Never stop asking to be shown the answers that you seek. Sometimes—and in my case, most often, it seems—He only shows me the very next step, just when I need it and often not more than that. It's like walking on a tightrope, but I trust Him completely. He's never let us down yet even when things have been at their worst." She smiled at Gigi. "And believe me when I say that we've had some hard times around here." She stroked the hair of the little girl in her lap. "But the kids know how much I love them. They know that they are safe and that, no matter what, they'll always have someone looking out for them."

"Do you have a lot of adoptions going through?" So far, what Gigi had seen here seemed so unlike the orphanage that she'd just come from that the questions about the kids being adopted and leaving seemed oddly out of place.

"No. Actually most of the children here cannot be adopted. There's a lot of red tape in this country when it comes to adopting—well, I'm sure you're probably somewhat aware of that, as it's no different for Place of Hope. But they have the kids who are eligible to be adopted."

Gigi guessed that the confusion probably showed on her face, as Silvia continued to explain.

"Many of the children who live here do have a living parent who gave them up, but hasn't signed away their rights to the child. So they are not eligible for adoption. So here, we just care for them for as long as they need us. Many will go on to get jobs or even work here at the orphanage. We've had a few who have even gone on to university, which we're quite proud of."

"That's so great. I can see why Tori was so taken with you all here," Gigi said.

"Tori's been a godsend to me—definitely a case of God bringing someone to help just when I needed it the most. We'll really miss her around here."

"Oh? I didn't realize that she was leaving."

"Well, she believes that she'll be back soon. She has some things back home to attend to." Silvia tousled the hair of the little girl stirring awake in her lap. "And we know that God will provide more help for us, isn't that right, Maria?"

Gigi tried to hide the worry that she felt on her face, but Silvia reached out to take her hand.

"Now don't you worry, Gigi. We're fine here—more than fine. We've actually got some great volunteers at the moment, of which you and Douglas are my new favorites." She winked. "Besides, we may just win you over for a longer stay before the week is done."

Gigi saw the gleam in Silvia's eye and knew that she was teasing, but she couldn't help the stirring that she felt in her heart—that feeling that was starting to become quite familiar to her now.

"Well, we do feel that we need to honor our commitment to Loretta and Frank, but who knows after that? Stranger things have happened." Gigi laughed and Silvia got up from the bed, placing Maria down to walk as she reached to take the baby from Gigi.

"I can keep her here for awhile if you don't mind." Gigi looked down at the sleeping child in her arms. "She looks so peaceful."

Silvia bent down to place a soft kiss on the baby's forehead. "She does, yes. She likes you." She grinned at Gigi. "And I was only joking about the 'winning you over' comment—well, mostly joking." She laughed. "I really just appreciate you being here and will look forward to spending more time with you throughout the week. I have the feeling that you're going to fit right in around here."

"I think so too. It already feels pretty good to me," Gigi said, looking down at the baby asleep in her arms.

Silvia turned just before she stepped outside the small room. "Dinner will be around six-thirty, and not that you have to feel like working so soon after arriving or anything, but feel free to join us earlier—if you'd like to help."

Gigi nodded her head. "You can count on it."

"Oh, and if you need some relief with the baby before then, bring her across to the main building. There will be someone to watch her there—a volunteer or one of the older children."

"Thank you. I will. Silvia?"

Silvia turned around to face her from just outside the open door.

"I'm glad that we're here—that we've met you. It feels very right to me." Gigi was trying to hold back some of her emotion.

Silvia grinned as she walked back across the room, making her way to where Gigi still sat on the mattress holding the baby. She reached down to give Gigi a big hug. When she finally released her embrace several seconds later, she looked Gigi intently in the eyes before she spoke. "It feels right to me too."

CHAPTER 19

Gigi sat on the mattress holding the baby girl long after Silvia had left the room. There was a nice breeze blowing through the open doorway, and she could hear the sounds of children's laughter from not very far away. The child stirred in her arms, and Gigi looked down just in time to see a big smile come across her face when she looked up to see who was holding her.

"Hi there, pretty girl." Gigi put her face close to the baby, smiling widely as she spoke to her. "I didn't even get your name, did I?" The little girl looked at her with wide eyes, making the sounds that only a delighted baby can make—sounds that can soften even the hardest of hearts—not that Gigi needed any warming up to at all by small children. It was a role that she was more than comfortable with—a role that she'd been missing desperately. "We'll just call you bella for now, won't we?" The baby giggled, seemingly delighted with the conversation.

Gigi tilted her own head back as she laughed, and

when she glanced up, she saw Douglas standing in the doorway. "Hey, you. How long have you been standing there?"

He had a habit of catching her off guard every once in a while when she would find him watching her, that smile on his face, his eyes filled with the love that she'd never tire of appreciating.

"Oh, long enough to witness one of the loveliest interactions that I've seen in a long time." He laughed as he crossed the small room to sit down on the mattress next to Gigi and the little girl, reaching his finger down for the baby to grasp. "Hi there, little one. Are you having fun?"

Gigi looked at him, feeling the big grin that didn't seem to leave her face these past few days. "Isn't she beautiful? And she seems so happy."

Douglas reached over to give Gigi a quick kiss on the cheek. "She does. And so do you."

"I am. I'm so happy. Holding this little one in my arms—well, it's exactly what I imagined it would be. Look at her. She just wants to be held, talked to, loved."

"All things that you are extremely skilled at, my darling," Douglas teased, winking at her and settling in beside her with his back against the wall.

"Well, babies are easy to love." She teased him back but only for a second before she reached out her hand to grasp his on his lap. "And adoring husbands. They're pretty easy to love too."

They both laughed, and Douglas was quiet beside her as he watched Gigi talk and coo with the little girl, the baby's giggling plenty of entertainment for both of them for the next several minutes.

"Do you regret not having children, Gigi?" Douglas's voice was quiet.

She thought for a few seconds before answering him. Of course it was a topic that they'd discussed before, but she sensed that he was seeing something different in her here—probably the same intense feeling that she was having but couldn't quite grasp herself.

"You know, the truth is, I think I do regret it. For many years, looking after Arianna was enough for me. I didn't even really think about the fact that I was unmarried, that those years of having children of my own were passing me by. And I suppose by the time I'd been with the Sinclairs for so long, I thought that I'd be a grandmother of sorts to Ari's children. So yes, I guess if I'm being honest, I wish that I did have my own grandchildren to look after, to love."

Douglas brought her hand up to his lips, a gesture Gigi never tired of. Her eyes filled with tears as she looked at him, and it was all she could do to speak.

"Do you regret it? Not having children?"

Gigi knew most of Douglas's history long before the two of them became involved because of his close friendship with the Sinclairs. She'd known the terrible time that he'd gone through watching his first wife lose her battle with cancer. And before she'd gotten sick, Douglas had been extremely focused on his career as a prominent lawyer in San Francisco. He and Gigi had talked about the fact that he'd not been willing to sacrifice the time needed for a child, that it had been a source of frustration between him and his wife. And then everything became about her illness. Gigi guessed that Douglas did have regrets, but they were different from her own.

"I don't think about it much, but I suppose if I had to do it all over again, yes. I would have had children. But I'm not sure that I would have been a great father."

Gigi caught the frown that appeared for just seconds on his face.

"I do think I would have been an excellent grandparent." He laughed, and Gigi guessed that he was probably trying to lighten the mood.

"Well, for the record, I think you would have been an excellent father. And you are most definitely a good grandpa."

Douglas laughed kissing her hand again. "Yes, we mustn't forget the girls. Jemma would never forgive us."

They had happily taken on the role of grandparents to Jemma and Kylie, and Gigi would always think of Blu as a daughter of sorts. Their easy relationship had evolved over the years, especially since Arianna's passing, and Gigi and Douglas knew that they were considered an extension of Blu's family.

Gigi looked at him for a moment as she adjusted the baby, who seemed to finally be getting slightly restless in her lap. "And also for the record…" She leaned over to kiss him on the lips. "I wouldn't change a thing if it meant not having you in my life right now."

He smiled at her and she thought she saw just the hint of a tear in his eye. "Me either."

Gigi held the baby out to Douglas. "Will you hold her for just a minute while I get up and use the restroom? I'm going to go early to help with dinner if you'd like to come. We can drop the baby off to someone on the way." She laughed. "Silvia sure does make everything sound so easy around here, but I gather that there's plenty of people to look after the little ones."

"Yes, I'll come with you." He stood up to take the little girl from Gigi. "I'm not sure how easy I'd say things are here but I think I know what you mean."

"Oh? I didn't even get a chance to hear about your walk—or to fill you in on the rest of my conversation with Silvia. Let's make sure to call it an early night so that we have plenty of time to talk."

Douglas nodded, his focus for the moment on the little girl he held in his arms.

PAULA KAY

CHAPTER 20

Everything had a very busy feel to it around the orphanage, and Gigi loved it. She and Douglas had found the building that Silvia had mentioned taking the baby to. Inside were more toddlers than Gigi had seen in long time. She laughed when she entered the room and saw the chaos that seemed loud but happy to her.

"Hi, I'm Kate. You must be Gigi and Douglas." A young girl stepped forward to greet them and take the baby out of Douglas's arms. "How is Gabriela feeling?"

"Gabriela. What a sweet name. We didn't know it until now, but she's been so good. I think her tummy must be feeling better, as she's hardly cried at all. And great to meet you, Kate." Gigi extended her hand to her. "This is quite a full room you have here." She laughed, looking around at the somewhat oddly organized busyness happening around her.

"Yes." Kate laughed too as she looked around the room. "Gabriela is our youngest right now. It would be more difficult with more babies, but actually the older girls help a lot with the younger kids." Kate gestured to one corner of the room where two older girls seemed to be working on a crafts project with the little ones. "They're wonderful, really. Have a look around if you like," Kate added with a big grin. "We'll all be heading over to the dining room shortly."

"That's where we're going after this," Gigi said as she walked over to say hello to the children and check out their project. She noticed Douglas's eyes darting around the room and she knew him well enough to know that he was assessing the quality of the building. She guessed that it was part of what he'd done earlier while out on his walk, and she knew that there would be discussions between them later about his assessment and what they might do to help the orphanage in terms of a donation.

The two said their goodbyes, with some hugs from the children and a last kiss to the smiling Gabriela, who seemed more than content with her new playmates for the night, and headed off to the dining room to see what they could do to help prepare for dinner.

There was a little clearing in the center of several buildings that were all within an easy distance of one another. As they walked along the path, Douglas pointed into the distance past the big building that Gigi guessed must be the dining room.

"The garden is back there and it's quite impressive, I must say—lots of variety, and it seems to be tended to very well."

Gigi nodded her head. "I'd love to have a proper look

tomorrow—get the full tour of the place. Right now it looks like someone is very happy to see you."

Before they'd made it to the dining room a young boy came running fast towards Douglas, his arms outstretched and a big grin on his face. Gigi guessed that he must have been about six or seven.

Douglas laughed, as he bent down to give the little boy the high five that he'd held his palm up for. "Gigi, this is Carlos."

Carlos grinned widely at Gigi. "Hola."

"Hola, Carlos. How old are you?"

"I am seven years old."

Gigi smiled at the expression of a child who was proud of his perfect English. "It's very nice to meet you." She smiled at Douglas, who had lifted the little boy onto his shoulders.

"I met Carlos when I was out walking earlier. He's the one who showed me the garden. And he's quite the tour guide, aren't you Carlos?"

"I don't understand, Mr. Doug."

Gigi and Douglas laughed at the confused but happy face smiling down at them.

"I was telling Gigi that you did a good job showing me around."

"Oh, yes. And more tomorrow, si?"

"Yes, tomorrow we want to see everything. Isn't that right, Gigi?"

Gigi nodded, reaching over to rub her hand across the

little boy's back. "Yes, that would be great, Carlos."

"Ms. Gigi?"

"Yes."

"That feels really good."

Gigi laughed because the wide smile and look on the child's face was priceless—like a cat that hadn't had a proper back scratch in ages.

"Well, aren't you just a very polite little boy?"

Carlos looked like he was debating whether or not to speak his thoughts out loud, which made Gigi even more amused. "Ms. Gigi."

"Yes."

"I'm actually almost eight years old." He looked so somber as he spoke that it was all Gigi could do to keep from laughing, but she kept herself composed as she replied to his rather serious statement.

"Oh, I'm sorry. You're not a little boy at all, are you then?"

"No. I'm a bit small for my age, but Ms. Silvia says I'll get bigger if I keep eating very well."

"Yes, that's right." Gigi smiled, but the thought also crossed her mind that she had noticed that many of the children did seem rather small for their age. She and Douglas would have to sit down with Silvia and make sure that they were getting the nutrition and calories that they needed. That would be priority number one in terms of the financial help that they could offer. Nothing was more important than that.

Gigi and Douglas, with Carlos on Douglas's shoulders, walked up to the dining room. It was a large area with a cement floor, and Gigi guessed that there were about twenty picnic-sized tables throughout. In fact, the area reminded her of what she'd seen at some of the big parks back home. There weren't walls except for the one at the far end, but the whole area was covered. To Gigi, it looked practical, while at the same time inviting.

The older kids were busy setting the tables, singing to the music playing from a large boom box in the corner, and before she could step further inside the room she felt little arms coming around her middle from behind, which made her instantly smile.

"Hola, Ms. Gigi," a quiet voice said.

Gigi turned around to scoop up the smiling Jimena into her arms. "Hola, Jimena. How are you?"

"I'm hungry." The child said it with an expression on her face that made both Gigi and Douglas laugh.

"Well, I bet you're going to be eating dinner very soon." Gigi set her down and took her by the hand. "Shall we go see if there's something we can help with?"

Jimena shook her head. "I have to help set the tables." Her expression grew quite serious again. "It's my chore."

Gigi laughed. "Okay. You go do that and you can sit by me at dinner if you like. Would that be good?"

"Si." Jimena grinned and then ran off towards the tables.

"Mr. Doug?"

Douglas had taken Carlos off his shoulders and the little boy was beside him, tugging on his shirt lightly as he spoke to get his attention.

"Yeah, buddy?" Douglas said, grinning as he put his hand around the small boy's shoulders.

"Can I sit by you at dinner?"

Gigi loved the interaction and the expression on her husband's face. Everything that had happened up until now was worth it for the experiences they were having. She'd never quite seen him this way with a child before and it was incredibly endearing to her.

"I'd like that very much, Carlos," Douglas said, giving the child a big smile to match his own. "Now should you be helping with the tables also?"

Carlos nodded, his eyes wide. "Si. I have to go do my chores too."

"Okay then. You come by us for dinner in a little while."

"I will. Adios, Mr. Doug." Carlos put his arms around Douglas's waist to give him a big squeeze before he took off running in the same direction that Jimena had gone. He stopped and turned as if he'd forgotten something. "Adios, Ms. Gigi. It was very nice meeting you." His grin was wide, and Gigi called out a goodbye as she reached over to put her arm around her husband.

Douglas leaned towards her to kiss her on the lips. "What a sweet kid."

"Yes, and I think he's taken quite a liking to you, Mr. Doug," Gigi teased, kissing him again. "Douglas?"

"Yes, love."

"Are we going to be able to leave them in a week?"

She meant it as a joke but the look they shared said it all.

"It might be hard, huh?" Douglas laughed.

"Yes, I think so."

"Well, let's not worry about that now, okay, honey? We have a full week ahead of us and I'm pretty sure that there's a lot to be done around here. I think we'll be earning our keep." He winked, and Gigi laughed as she hugged him to her.

"Well, aren't you two the picture of a young couple in love over here in the corner?" Tori teased them with a wide smile as she walked up with Rafael right behind her, both of them carrying large buckets.

"I don't know about young, but I'll take the 'in love' bit of your comment." Douglas took Gigi's hand and looked her in the eyes. "This one's easy to fall in love with every day."

Gigi felt her face getting warm at the compliment and hoped that their displays of affection were not too much. She made a mental note to ask Tori about it later, wanting to be sure that they weren't committing some big faux pas with their small kisses and hand holding around the children.

It was something that had taken Gigi a bit to get used

to when they'd begun dating. Douglas was very affectionate and since she'd hardly dated, it was all a bit much for her at the beginning. But she'd grown more and more comfortable, and by the time they were married it was one of the things that she loved most about her adoring husband. She never tired of it and rarely felt embarrassed by it now.

Tori's laughter brought Gigi out of her thoughts. "Douglas, would you mind going to get water with Rafael? There's a well not far down the path there." She pointed beyond where they'd come from.

Douglas took the two buckets from Tori. "I'd be happy to."

"Thank you." Tori turned to Gigi. "And do you want to come with me? I'll show you where Silvia and the others are making tortillas." She grinned widely. "Nothing like jumping right in, huh?"

Gigi reached over to give her a quick hug. "Oh, Tori. I'm so glad we came—so happy that we met you." She couldn't help the tears that were just beginning to come to the surface again. It was just all so surreal at times.

Tori hugged her back. "I'm so glad too. I think it was absolutely the right decision for you two, and I'm glad that you don't have any regrets—so far." She laughed lightly. "We'll see how you feel after your first night on that mattress."

Gigi laughed at Tori's joke as she followed her to the far side of the dining room, knowing that she could have the worst night's sleep ever and still not feel an ounce of regret.

PAULA KAY

CHAPTER 21

Gigi looked around her as she helped to shape the corn tortillas into little patties. She loved the busy, slightly chaotic nature of what she'd seen of the orphanage so far. Being in the kitchen area, which really only involved the very back of the dining room, was no different. Tori had introduced her to the main cook, Fernanda, a local woman who had been working there for the past seven years. Fernanda had explained in her broken English that Casa de los Niños had opened up their clinic to the local people as well as the school, where her young son attended. In exchange for his education and a small local wage, she was happy to help out at the orphanage in any way that she could. It had become a second home for her and her son.

Gigi loved hearing more about the local families as she worked alongside Fernanda, learning how the fresh tortillas were made and that they were a staple for the kids for most meals. Behind Gigi and Fernanda, Silvia and Tori were making beans and what Gigi thought smelled like a delicious sort of stew with chicken. The women laughed easily with one another, dancing to the music that still played from the boom box in the corner. Silvia had one small toddler on her hip as she cooked and another right beside her—a sight that Gigi thought was probably the norm around here when it came to Silvia.

"So, Gigi. What do you think of our little crew?" Silvia's voice interrupted Gigi's thoughts.

Gigi gave her a wide smile. "I absolutely love it. Thanks so much for having us."

"Are you kidding? Don't thank me. It's you I'll be thanking when the week is over." Silvia laughed. "I think that you're going to find yourself quite busy around here."

"That is more than fine by us. We're both looking forward to digging in and helping out however we can."

Gigi looked up from the tortillas on the stove as she heard her husband's voice—"We have come bearing drink."

Silvia said, "Great, thanks, you two. Rafael, can you please go ahead and start with the water for the kids?"

"Sure, Ms. Silvia," Rafael said, taking his bucket over to a table where the plastic cups were stacked high.

"What do you think of our well?" Silvia directed her question towards Douglas.

"It's great. And it serves your needs just fine?"

"Si. We used to have to walk a good two miles or so—there's another well for the local villages a bit further into the jungle. Last year an organization from Canada came in to install the well for us. It's really been a godsend—one of many things that have helped this place to run better over the past few years." Silvia put the little boy she'd been holding down on his feet so that she could start scooping up the beans onto the plates being held by a line of older kids who'd suddenly appeared.

Gigi marveled once again at how everyone seemed to work so well together. The plates were filled with food, and the kids started distributing them to the tables now filling with kids.

"Ana, would you ring the bell for dinner, please?" Silvia called out to one of the children in the dining room. "We try to keep to a schedule for meals, but it doesn't always work that way," she explained to Gigi. "We'll have a few stragglers coming in now, but most of the kids will be starving by this time." She winked.

Gigi must have had a concerned expression on her face, because Silvia quickly added, "Oh, I don't mean starving as in not getting enough food—just that they've been playing and working hard all day—you know, building up a good appetite." She laughed. "Gigi, if you can just hand out the last of those tortillas, then why don't you and Douglas fix yourselves a plate and go ahead and sit wherever you like? You'll see the other volunteers sitting at different tables with the little ones, and I'm sure they'd love to meet you before the night is over too."

Gigi and Douglas took their plates over to a table where Jimena, Carlos, and a few other kids were sitting. The two looked up with big grins on their faces when they saw them approaching the table.

"I saved you a spot by me, Mr. Doug." Carlos patted the seat next to him. "And I got you some water already too." He looked over at Gigi. "And you, Ms. Gi."

Jimena looked across the table at Carlos with wide eyes as she whispered. "Carlos, it's Ms. Gigi, not Ms. Gi."

Gigi and Douglas laughed at the little exchange as Gigi bent over to give Jimena a quick kiss on the head. "It's okay. Some of my favorite people call me Gi." For just a moment, she flashed to Arianna and what would have been a typical exchange between them. If only Arianna could see her now. Gigi laughed lightly as she thought about what the young girl would have thought about how she and Douglas were spending their time right now. Even back then, Arianna was always scolding her for not taking the time to do the things that she wanted to do.

Douglas had a question on his face as she caught his eye across the table. Gigi explained:

"I was just thinking about Arianna—what she'd think if she could see us now."

"Who's Arianna?" Carlos said.

"Arianna was a very special friend of ours." Douglas said as he looked down at Carlos and then back over at Gigi. "She was one of those people who used to call Gigi Gi."

"Is Arianna going to come visit us too?" Jimena looked up at Gigi.

"No, honey. Arianna's in heaven."

Gigi saw the look pass between Carlos and Jimena. "What is it, honey?" Gigi directed towards Carlos.

"Jimena's mommy went to heaven too. Ms. Silvia says that she's looking down on Jimena every day—even right now, right, Jimena?"

Jimena nodded and seemed thoughtful for a moment. "Ms. Gigi?"

"Yes, honey?"

"I wonder if mommy knows Arianna."

Gigi tried hard to hold back the tears that threatened. "I bet she does, sweetie. I bet that they're good friends and both looking down on us right now."

Jimena smiled and looked up at Gigi. "That makes me really happy."

Gigi leaned down to give the little girl another quick kiss on the forehead. "It makes me really happy too, honey."

And across the table she saw Douglas take a quick swipe of his eyes with his hand, shaking his head, but there was no mistaking the look on his face. They were being changed already here at Casa de los Niños, and it hadn't even been a full day yet.

CHAPTER 22

They finished their dinner and, like clockwork again, everyone pitched in to help. Some of the older children and one of the volunteers had taken the little ones back to get ready for bed, while the others stayed in the dining room, clearing the tables and starting in on the dishes.

Gigi smiled when she saw Silvia walking towards her, one toddler on her hip, another by her side.

"So, after we clean up from dinner, the kids will get ready for bed and then we'll all meet outside by the big fire pit if you'd like to join us. I'm sure you must be tired, so don't feel obligated. I'd love it if you could get an early start with us tomorrow." She flashed a big grin their way. "And tomorrow I'm going to give you the full tour of the place."

"That sounds great. I'm sure we can manage a few more hours before bed." Gigi laughed, looking over at Douglas, who was nodding his head. "We'll just help you with the dishes right now."

"That's great, thanks. Usually it goes pretty fast around here. The kids are so good about pitching in—

well, they know that it's how we do business." Silvia laughed, and Gigi thought again how much she admired the way that things were run around the orphanage.

It was so different from what their experience had been at Place of Hope. She tried to push the thought aside, reminding herself that she didn't want to be comparing the two places. Well, there was no comparison, really. Hands down, Casa de los Niños had been the experience she'd been looking for all those months ago. Thank goodness they'd met Tori. Once again, she marveled at how everything had happened.

Gigi stifled a yawn as she and Douglas entered their little hut. "That was so much fun, wasn't it?"

They had spent the evening by the fire watching the kids sing and dance. Then when it was time to put the little ones to bed, they'd helped to tuck them in, reading stories and singing songs. The whole evening had been the perfect way to end their first night there.

"It was fun, darling." Douglas leaned over to give her a quick kiss. "You really love those kids already, don't you?"

There was something in the way he asked the question that reminded Gigi of his continued promise to make her happy. How did she get so lucky? Douglas had been more than her knight in shining armor, much more than any man she ever could have dreamt up to be her husband.

"I do, honey." She looked at him knowing that he'd guess the question in her eyes before she even spoke it. "Do you?"

Douglas nodded slowly. "I must admit that little Carlos, that rascal, seems to have nipped at a bit of my heart."

Gigi laughed. "Like a puppy, you mean?"

"No. That's not what I mean." He laughed as he sat down next to where Gigi sat on the bed. "He's a really great kid. They all are."

"You sound surprised."

"I am, if I'm being honest. I expected that the kids would take to you right away, of course. It's what I was most looking forward to as we took the journey to come here. I didn't really expect to be that affected by them myself."

Gigi reached over for Douglas's hand. "I know what you mean. I still can't believe that it's only our first day. I'm really looking forward to the week. Are you?"

"Yes. I'm anxious to get that tour tomorrow. I want to do a thorough assessment of the place so that we know what their repair needs are and all of their needs in general. I'm sure Silvia will let us know also when we have a big talk with her."

"I'm sure that she will. And I'm with you on looking forward to the tour. I feel like we've just scratched the surface around here and I'm anxious to see more—where the kids go to school and how a normal day looks for them."

Gigi yawned and Douglas pulled her in for a big hug. "Why don't you get ready for bed, love? We should really get a good night's rest. I'm pretty sure that they start their day early around here."

Gigi nodded as she got up from the bed to change. Ten seconds later, with a scream, she was back on top of the bed.

"What is it?" Douglas jumped up, startled at her quick reaction.

Gigi was trying not to be overly dramatic now that her heart had quit racing a bit. "A mouse. Over by the sink."

Douglas laughed lightly. "Honey?

"Yes?" Gigi said from under the covers that she'd now snuggled down into.

"I'm sorry to tell you that we might end up seeing more than a mouse around here during our stay."

Gigi laughed lightly, taking a deep breath. "It's okay."

"It's okay? Who are you and what alien has inhabited my wife's body?"

Gigi laughed. "Come in the bed by me, mister."

Douglas obeyed, quickly changing out of his clothes and snuggling under the covers with his wife. "Is that better?" he said, his arms wrapped around Gigi, his lips nuzzled into the back of her neck.

"It's perfect, honey." Gigi knew he couldn't see the big grin on her face, but she thought that maybe she'd never felt more content than in this moment.

A moment later she heard a little flurry of activity from the corner of the room.

"Honey?"

"Yes?"

"Are you going to be able to sleep tonight?"

Gigi reached down to place her hand on top of his, the one holding her close to him. "Yes, I'm going to sleep very well, darling. Everything is as it should be and I couldn't feel more at home. Even with our little friend sharing our space with us." She laughed lightly. "Good night."

Douglas snuggled in closer and gave the back of her neck another quick kiss. "Sleep well. I love you."

Gigi knew she'd be drifting off to sleep within minutes, a smile of contentment on her face, the man whom she loved holding her tight.

PAULA KAY

CHAPTER 23

Gigi stirred on the mattress, looking up at Douglas, who was sitting in bed reading.

"What is that?" she said of the loud noise that had woken her up.

"Oh, you mean our early morning rooster alarm?"

She listened intently as a few more crows erupted into the otherwise silent outdoors. "You know, I kinda like it. Feels a little less intrusive than the alarm clock, doesn't it?"

Douglas laughed as he reached for her hand to give it a quick kiss. "I like it too. Are you awake? Come sit here by me."

Gigi pulled herself up so that she was sitting with her back against the wall. "Yes, I feel ready to start my day. I keep seeing Jimena's face in my head. I can't wait to see that little sweetie this morning."

"I know what you mean," Douglas said, leaning over to give Gigi a kiss. "I must admit that having Carlos around was really growing on me too." He laughed. "I think they will both be in school today, though. Or at least I'm pretty sure that's what Silvia was saying when she talked about giving us the tour."

Gigi nodded. "I think so too, but I get the feeling that there's a little leeway around here, so don't be surprised if your little buddy turns up today." She smiled and was thoughtful for a moment before she continued. "So we never really discussed your thoughts from yesterday—when you came back from your walk."

"Or the rest of your conversation with Silvia either," Douglas said. "It sure does feel like we've been here more than just one day."

"Yes, it's funny, isn't it?" Gigi was quiet for a minute. "What are you thinking, honey?"

"Oh, I just hope the week doesn't go so fast."

Douglas looked at her, seeming to study her expression for a few minutes before answering. "Darling, we can't worry about that now. Let's just enjoy the week."

"I agree. So tell me about what you did see yesterday."

"Oh, right. So I didn't get a chance to walk around everywhere—I'm sure we'll see more today. But so many of the buildings seem to need pretty serious repairs, if that's even enough, to be honest. It might actually be safest to tear down most of these buildings and rebuild from the ground up."

"I know what you mean. I saw you really scrutinizing the kids' dorm last night when we were there. It's pretty bad, isn't it?"

"It is in my opinion. I'd say we start with that one for sure. I'll talk more about it today with Silvia. I'm sure she doesn't realize just how bad it really could be. But we've got to make sure that it's safe where those kids are sleeping and spending so much of their time."

"That's an easy thing we can do, right, honey? Donate a new dormitory for the kids?"

"Yes, definitely."

"Hmm."

Douglas asked, "Hmm what?"

"I was just thinking—if you don't mind, let's earmark the dorm donation from some of Ari's money. Would that be okay with you?"

Gigi and Douglas had long since combined all of their finances, but when it came to the inheritance that Arianna had left Gigi, he was firm that the money should remain separate for Gigi to decide what to do with it. He had built up enough retirement savings and had enough investments that he and Gigi could live out the rest of their years on that income alone, so there was never really an issue about needing to tap into the inheritance money.

Douglas brought Gigi's hand up to his lips. "I think that's a great idea, love."

"I just think that she would have really liked to be a part of this—to do something pretty great for these kids."

Gigi looked at Douglas, who had a very funny expression on his face. "What's that face for?"

"Well, I'm just trying to picture Ari here—at the

orphanage." He laughed. "Not really the Arianna that I knew."

Gigi laughed too. "You're right. It would have been way out of her comfort zone for sure." Gigi was quiet for a few seconds. "But you know what?"

Douglas nodded for her to continue.

"I have to wonder…Arianna had changed so much—at the end, I mean. I'll be the first to admit that she was very much a spoiled little rich girl for most of her life. But I'd like to think that at the end—if she'd had more time, I mean—she would have actually come to a place like this. And I know that she would have cared about these kids, even if she couldn't have handled sleeping on a mattress in a hut—"

"—with a mouse in the corner of the room," Douglas interrupted, winking at her. "I know what you mean and I agree with you. Ari had changed. A lot, actually." He leaned over to kiss her. "And I do think it's a great idea—to donate the building in Ari's honor."

The two sat for a few more minutes, each lost in their own thoughts as the roosters crowed and the morning light started to show through the worn curtains of the small windows of the hut.

Stepping outside a little while later, Gigi was surprised to see how much the weather had changed.

"Wow, it looks like we might have a storm coming our way." Douglas said what Gigi had been thinking as he looked up at the dark sky. "I wonder how equipped they are to deal with a lot of rain."

"I guess we'll find out soon enough, by the looks of that sky."

The two rushed over to the dining hall to get started with the breakfast preparations.

"Hi, how did you two sleep your first night?" Tori greeted them with a smile on her face as she stirred something in a big pot on the stove.

"Great." Gigi returned the smile.

"Well, we do seem to have a little critter sharing our space with us." Douglas winked and then laughed at the look on Tori's face.

"Oh no. I can only imagine what that might be." Tori laughed. "I hope it hasn't changed your mind about staying."

"Not in the least," Gigi said, crossing over to give Tori a quick hug. "It was just a little mouse, nothing I haven't seen before." She looked into the three large pots that Tori had going on the stove. "What are you making there?"

"Oh, it's just a type of porridge. It will be good for a morning like today, I think. It got cold during the night, didn't it?"

"It did," Douglas said. "Looks like maybe we have a storm coming our way."

"Oh, speaking of—Silvia wanted me to be sure to tell you that she's sorry for missing you this morning. It looks like I'm going to be starting out with you on your tour today, and hopefully she'll be able to join us later."

"I hope everything's alright?" Gigi didn't know why exactly, but she felt a touch of worry.

"Oh, yes. Everything's fine. Silvia is worried about the kid's dorm. The roof needs to be patched and with the storm coming—"

"I assume that what you mean by that is that she has someone on the roof fixing it for her?" Douglas said, and the look of concern on his face did not go unnoticed by Gigi.

Tori looked like she wasn't sure quite how to respond to Douglas's question.

"I know, I know, Douglas. It's not ideal, but Silvia's not one to wait around when something needs to be done."

"This is not going to be okay with me. Either I'm going to get up there or we'll get someone else to do it. I'm not going to have Silvia up there where it's not safe. That's the last thing the kids need, right? Silvia with a broken leg?"

Tori was nodding her head, and Gigi was quick to interject.

"Honey, I don't want you getting up there either. I'm sure we can get someone in to help."

Tori was laughing a bit and Gigi guessed she was trying to lighten the mood. "Listen, you two, we don't need to worry about this right this minute. Silvia's off to get some supplies. Yes, it is an issue of timing because of the storm coming. That's all. But if we have to, we can manage with the kids in the other buildings tonight, so let's not worry about it until we talk to Silvia later, deal?"

"Deal." Douglas winked. "Sorry to give you a hard time about it. I know you're only the messenger, so to speak."

"Well, it's just that I know Silvia well—how she operates around here. If there's something to be done and she can do it herself, it's hard to stop her—safe or not."

"I get that from the little bit of time I've spent with her too," Gigi said. "And I understand Douglas's concern." Gigi walked over to put her arm around her husband. She loved that he was always so concerned about others. She'd never fault him for trying to assert himself when she knew that it had do with the well-being of another person. She suspected that he and Silvia might end up butting heads a bit over such things before they left, but maybe Silvia would surprise them all if she were given some other options—options that Gigi and Douglas wanted to let her know about sooner rather than later.

The morning chatter of the children filing into the dining area interrupted any serious talk among the three for the time being. Gigi and Douglas helped to get all of the children served and then found their place among a group of kids that they'd not yet gotten a chance to speak with.

Gigi was quite surprised that most of the kids seemed to have a pretty good grasp of English. When Douglas asked one of the older boys about their studies, he told the couple all about Ms. Pamela, their teacher, who was also from America. All of the children nodded their heads, loudly proclaiming how much they liked school and Ms. Pamela.

Douglas winked at Gigi while the kids chattered around them, and she knew that he was probably having a thought similar to her own. Silvia was doing a lot of things right around here. And the team that she had helping her might be small, but they seemed to be highly effective in the way that they were running things and in the positive impact that they were having on these children.

"Ms. Gigi."

Gigi heard a quiet voice behind her at the same time that she felt a little hand on her back. She turned around, knowing before doing so that the sweet voice belonged to Jimena.

"Good morning, lovely girl." Gigi turned her body around on the bench where she sat so that she could reach out to give the little girl a hug, but Jimena beat her to it, wrapping her arms tightly around Gigi's neck the moment she turned around at the table.

Gigi laughed and gave the little girl a quick kiss on the cheek. "Did you want to sit here and eat your breakfast with us?"

"Yes, please."

Gigi lifted her onto the bench to sit beside her, winking at Douglas, who seemed to be enjoying the interaction across the table from where he sat.

Before long the other volunteers had whisked the children off to brush their teeth and get ready for a day of school. Gigi and Douglas were helping with the clean-up, and then Tori was going to give them the tour that they had been anticipating since their arrival. Gigi felt that she had a very good idea of the orphanage, but they still hadn't seen the school and a few of the other main areas in action.

CHAPTER 24

Gigi and Douglas were following Tori as they made their way to the big garden beyond the dining hall.

"So, they've had this garden for about ten years now. Some volunteers put it in as a big project and it, along with the cows and chickens we have now, has helped immensely in terms of the food budget for the orphanage."

Gigi was nodding her head as she looked around at the well-kept space of land. There was a large-sized field of corn growing just beyond that, and she could see where the cows and chickens were kept.

"Some of the older kids help out with the gardening, and we do have one local person that is our main source of help when it comes to the garden and the animals."

"I think it's really great that the kids play such an active role in everything around here," Douglas said.

"Yes, the kids know that we're just one big family, and in families, everyone pitches in to help," Tori said, flashing a wide grin. "Let's head over to the kids' dorm now, and maybe Silvia will be about ready to join us."

Tori's eyes went to the sky. "I'm not sure how much more time we have before the rain comes."

Douglas took Gigi's hand as they followed Tori towards the kids' dorm. She could feel his grip tightening on her hand as they got closer and she could make out that Silvia was on the roof of the building.

"Oh, God," Douglas said under his breath.

"Honey, just remember that Silvia isn't used to having a lot of options around here. At least I don't think so, is that right, Tori?"

"Yes, exactly. I have to really admire her. And I always will. I've never seen a more hardworking woman."

"Well, she might be all those things, but I'm not ever going to be comfortable with her up on an unstable roof like that."

Gigi looked at Tori and shrugged her shoulders as Douglas walked ahead of them over to the building, below where Silvia was pounding nails into the roof.

As they got closer, they could hear what Silvia was saying to Douglas as she got ready to climb down the ladder.

"Oh, I'm fine. And I'm finished now. Well, not finished, but it will hold for now. I hope." She laughed lightly as she made her way down the ladder.

"Yeah, and if you should fall? Honestly, it's not worth it," Douglas said.

Gigi saw a look on Silvia's face that she'd not seen before. "Oh, it's worth it. The kids are always worth it to me." She took a deep breath as if trying to pull pack on the anger that seemed about to erupt.

Oh, she's a mama bear, Gigi thought to herself. Ready to defend her cubs always. She couldn't help but smile as she watched the exchange between Silvia and her husband. She loved the woman's passion for the kids most of all.

"I'm sorry, Silvia. I just meant that—if something happened to you—well, the kid's would be worse off, that's all."

Silvia leaned over to give Douglas a quick peck on the cheek. "It's okay. I know what you meant. I don't worry about such things, Douglas. God is looking out for me and if something were to happen, well—I trust that it's all in His time." She grinned. "That's all. In the meantime, I'm what the kids have, so if a roof needs to be patched to keep them dry, so be it." She laughed. "Anyways, I'm done now. It's not perfect but I think it will hold for tonight."

They all walked around the building to enter the dorm, and Gigi could hear Douglas up ahead with Silvia telling her about their desire to have a new dorm built right away. She smiled when Silvia stopped to give first Douglas, and then Gigi, a big hug.

"Thank you both. That's a wonderful gesture, and one that the kids and I appreciate very much."

Douglas caught Gigi's eye and she nodded for him to continue. "Silvia, we'd like to do much more. After the tour, if you have some time, Gigi and I would like to sit down with you to go over some things."

"And we'd like to tell you about a friend of ours," Gigi said as she reached over to give Silvia a hug. She wanted Silvia to know the full story about the large donation that they were going to make. She wanted a chance to tell her about Arianna.

CHAPTER 25

Gigi sat with Carlos by her side, the music loud and the children's laughter even louder. Her gaze went to Douglas, out on the makeshift dance floor with Jimena in his arms, her head thrown back as she laughed and sang to a tune that the kids seemed to know by heart. The children had wanted to throw them a party on their last night, and she couldn't have thought up a better way to end the time that they'd had at Casa de los Niños.

Her eyes filled with tears as she thought about the week that they'd had and leaving the kids that she'd grown to love. It had all gone so fast. They'd worked hard alongside Silvia and the volunteers, but they'd also played a lot more than probably any other time in their adult lives. She smiled as she remembered the conversation that she'd had with Douglas that morning when they talked about leaving. She believed it had been one of the best times of her life and not something that she'd forget any time soon. Douglas had commented that she'd never looked happier and he couldn't believe the difference that the kids had made in her life. He'd even promised her that they'd try to get back one more time, after they finished at Place of Hope.

She watched him now, Jimena still in his arms and Carlos now by his side as they walked towards the refreshment table for some food. It had been rare during the whole week to see Douglas without Carlos nearby. The little boy had taken such a liking to Douglas, and she'd not ever seen him grow so close to a child so fast. Even though he hadn't expressed it as fully as Gigi had, she knew that he had to be feeling some sadness about leaving the little boy—about leaving all of them.

Her thoughts were interrupted by the plate of snacks that Carlos thrust into her hands, while at the same time Jimena did her best to find space on Gigi's lap without sitting on top of the food.

"Hold on there, kids." Gigi laughed, placing the plate of food by her side so that the child could sit on her lap. "You sure look like you're having fun out there on the dance floor."

"It's so fun. I love the music, don't you, Ms. Gi?" Carlos said, his grin wide.

Gigi nodded her head as Jimena quickly interjected.

"Mr. Doug is a very good dancer." Her eyes shone, and Gigi watched her husband look over at the small girl.

"As are you, my dear," he said, causing her grin to grow even wider.

"I don't want you to leave," Carlos said suddenly.

And when Gigi turned towards him she could see the tears streaming down his face as he looked at Douglas.

Douglas looked like he was holding back some sudden emotion himself as he scooped the boy into his lap, something the child hadn't always been agreeable to, but he didn't resist it now.

"I know. Gigi and I are sad that we're leaving too, but you know what?"

"What?"

"We're going to come back again in a few weeks—to see you before we go home to the U.S."

"You are?" Jimena's eyes were wide. "I don't want you to leave either." She leaned her head down against Gigi's chest, and as Gigi looked at Douglas over the child's head, she felt her heart breaking.

"Mr. Doug?" Carlos's tears had stopped and the look on his face seemed very serious as he looked up at Douglas.

"Yes?"

"Can I call you Papa Doug?"

Gigi couldn't stop the tears, and just as quickly, Douglas was swiping at his eyes with his hand, pulling the little boy in for a hug. "Yes, Carlos. You sure can, buddy."

It was Douglas's turn to glance over at Gigi, and the look on his face with the tears coming now said it all.

Casa de los Niños had changed them both forever.

PAULA KAY

CHAPTER 26

The journey back to Antigua had been a quiet one.
Gigi had suddenly felt very tired once she was in the car
and her emotions were all over the place. Their goodbyes
on the dock that morning had been hard—much harder
than even she would have imagined a week ago. Her
thoughts turned towards the conversation that she'd had
with Silvia over breakfast.

"I have a strong feeling that you two will be back
soon," Silvia had said, giving Gigi a big hug.

Gigi had laughed, telling her about their plan to return
in a few weeks before they headed back home. And just
as quickly the mood between the two women had gotten
serious as Gigi told how much the time had meant to her
and Douglas, and just how much they thought of her.
Silvia's love and passion for the children and her life's
work was special—anyone who spent any amount of time
with her could see that—and Gigi deeply admired her for
it.

"Penny for your thoughts." Douglas leaned over to kiss her on the cheek, startling her back to the conversation that he'd been trying to have with her for the past few minutes.

"Oh, sorry, honey." Gigi smiled as she continued to unpack her clothes from the suitcase.

They'd been back at Place of Hope for a few hours and she needed to get her mind prepared for the week ahead.

"No worries, love. I was just wondering if you wanted to go with the volunteers to dinner. I met the new couple earlier and they mentioned that a group of them were going out to try a new restaurant later."

"You know, I'm not really that hungry. I think I'll just make a sandwich or something here. But you should go ahead if you want to." She flashed him a smile. She was trying to lighten her mood. She knew that no matter how upset she was feeling about leaving the jungle, she had to try to make the best of it while they were here.

"I'm not hungry either," Douglas said, coming over to put his arm around her waist. "I do think it might be interesting to catch up with the volunteers this week. I really can't believe that Sarah has left."

"I know. That surprised me as well. When I asked Loretta about it earlier, she said that Sarah had decided to move on with her travels. She didn't seem particularly bothered about it, so they must be feeling pretty organized with everything."

"We'll find out tomorrow, I guess." Douglas winked.

They'd promised Loretta that they would be around all week to help with whatever needed to be done. Gigi guessed there would be more stuffing envelopes, but maybe if she was lucky she could convince Loretta to let her spend some time with the older kids after their studies were done for the day. Without meaning to, she heard the sigh escape her lips.

"Are you going to be okay, darling?"

She hated making her husband worry about her.

"Oh yes. Never mind me. I'm going to be just fine." She laughed lightly, trying to put his mind at ease.

"Honey, we'll be back there before you know it—just two short weeks."

Gigi turned to reach her arms around Douglas's neck, pulling him in for a deep kiss. "I love you, you know." She pulled her head back to look him in the eyes. "Everything you've done for me—in coming here—it means everything."

She tried unsuccessfully to hold back her tears, and seconds later Douglas was reaching his finger across her cheek to wipe away the wetness.

"You mean everything to me." He kissed her.

PAULA KAY

CHAPTER 27

Over the course of the next week, Gigi and Douglas settled back into a routine at Place of Hope. They were the ones to oversee the kids getting ready for school in the mornings—Douglas had insisted to Loretta that Gigi should have more time to spend with the children. They would take care of the office-type tasks also, but that could be done while the kids were in school. Gigi also spent time with the children during their homework period and after, for the hour or so that they had free before dinner.

Gigi wasn't exactly unhappy—she loved the children at Place of Hope and spending time with them over the past week had been good for her. But her heart ached for Jimena, Carlos, and the other kids at Casa de los Niños. There was no denying how affected she'd been by her time in the jungle. She was beside herself with excitement about returning to visit soon, and in the meantime she wanted to be giving her best to the children at Place of Hope.

"Honey."

Gigi looked across the room to where Douglas sat at his computer. They'd just finished getting the kids settled at school and were contemplating a walk to Jess's cafe. They'd only been in a few times to see her since they'd returned from the jungle.

"Yes?" Gigi walked over to where Douglas sat, to lightly rub his back. "Do you want to go for a walk?"

She thought she saw a look of concern on his face as he turned around to look at her.

"I got an email from Tori earlier."

"How is she? The kids?" Gigi felt her whole face light up just thinking about Tori and the kids again.

"She says she's in town—at the cafe—just for the day." He took Gigi by the hand. "She says that she needs to see us right away."

"Hmm. I wonder what's up? Do you think we should be worried?"

Gigi felt her heart pounding; she knew something wasn't right even before she asked the question.

Douglas pulled her down onto his lap. "Yes. Something is wrong."

Gigi saw the worry on his face.

"When I replied asking her if everything was okay, she wrote back saying that it wasn't—and asked that we come to Jess's as soon as possible."

Gigi sighed. "I guess we better get going, then. As anxious as I am to see Tori, I'm now very concerned about what kind of news she has for us." She put her arms around Douglas's neck for a quick squeeze before getting up off his lap. "I wonder what it could possibly be."

God, I hope nothing has happened to one of the kids. She tried to brush the thought aside, willing herself to not think the worst as they quickly got their things together to head to the cafe.

Gigi stopped for a moment just outside the door to the cafe. She squeezed Douglas's hand that she'd been holding. There had been mostly silence between them during the walk over. Gigi guessed that they'd both been imagining the worst, but not wanting to say the words out loud. Now, as she stood looking through the window of the cafe, she could see Tori and Jess seated at a table in the corner. She took a deep breath and motioned for Douglas to open the door.

Tori was on her feet coming towards them just as soon as Douglas entered the cafe. Gigi saw her friend's face, eyes swollen and red, seconds before Tori had Gigi in an embrace—seconds before the sobs came, loud and furious.

Douglas came up beside them, lightly putting his hand on Tori's back as the tears came. Gigi looked over at Jess, busy getting some coffees, but Gigi didn't miss the tears being wiped from her eyes as she did so.

God, this is bad. Really bad.

Gigi held on to Tori, letting her cry as she looked towards Douglas, her heart pounding. They needed to find out what had happened.

"Tori, can you tell us what happened?" Douglas was asking in a quiet voice.

Gigi could feel Tori trying to control her sobs, and she guessed that she was trying to get the words out.

Finally, Tori stood back from Gigi, taking a deep breath.

"It's Silvia."

Gigi felt instant tears and her own sob catching in her throat.

"She fell off the roof yesterday morning."

Tori looked like she was trying very hard to hold it together—to deliver the news that Gigi knew was coming next.

More sobs from Tori and another deep breath as she looked at Douglas, then Gigi. "She died instantly."

Gigi felt Tori's arms around her as her whole body went weak, her own sobs of shock and grief drowning out any other noise in the room. Douglas's hand on her shoulder barely registered as she felt him guiding her down into the chair nearby. She looked at him sitting next to her, his face wet with tears.

The four of them sat around the small table, crying and sipping the coffee that Jess had delivered to them. No one spoke for several minutes; Gigi felt completely overwhelmed by the news. But she knew that there was much more to be discussed. She looked at Tori, sitting across from her, a hundred questions running through her mind—questions she didn't know if she wanted the answers to.

Finally Tori spoke again, directing her words towards Douglas.

"Earlier yesterday morning, she'd laughed with me at breakfast. She told me—'Don't tell Douglas I'm on the roof.'" Tori's voice caught as she struggled to continue. "She'd joked about it—that she couldn't wait for someone else to do the job because there was another storm blowing in fast."

Gigi could see the question on Douglas's face before he spoke it.

"But I thought she'd already taken care of that?"

Gigi thought he looked angry, and she had a bad feeling in the back of her mind that somehow Douglas could end up blaming himself for this. She pushed the thought aside as Tori replied to Douglas's question.

Tori sighed. "It was a new area of the roof."

"I should have fixed it myself when I was there." Douglas was angry.

"Douglas, no. It wasn't for you to fix. And honestly, if it's not one thing, it's another around there that needs to be repaired. I know Silvia—I-I-knew her well, and—" Tori started crying again, unable to continue.

Douglas reached his hand across the table to grab Tori's. "I know. I know what you mean. She was stubborn about it. She wouldn't have waited to get something fixed that she thought she could do herself."

Gigi could hardly stand the thoughts that were going through her mind. "Who found her?"

Tori reached out to grasp Gigi's hand. "The children never saw her. It was Fernanda." Tori was still crying. "She'd just left the kitchen after breakfast clean-up when she heard the fall." She stopped to take a deep breath. "After she ran to her, she went to get help, but—but it was too late."

Gigi felt like she was in a state of shock. It was all so much to take in. Douglas seemed to be holding it together, but she knew that he was taking it hard as well. It was hard to believe that they'd seen Silvia not even a week earlier. With that thought came the image of Silvia with the kids—her babies, she'd often called them. Gigi couldn't help the loud sobs from coming again as she thought about the children and how much their lives would be changing now.

More time passed, much of it in silence as they each sat with their own thoughts—and grief. Finally, Tori asked Jess for the time, and got up from the table.

"I know this is all so sudden—and so much to take in. I'm sorry to give you all of this news in such a rush, but I need to get back to the kids today. And I was hoping—" She looked at Gigi and Douglas. "I was really hoping that you could come back—to help me with the kids—and with everything."

Gigi looked over at Douglas, counting on him to speak for both of them—which he did without hesitation as he got up from the table to give Tori a hug.

"Of course we will. We'll help you with whatever you need."

"Yes, we'll get through this together." Gigi agreed, also giving her friend a big hug.

"I've postponed my trip. I can't go right now. But I will have to very soon. I just—I don't know what's going to happen with the kids—with Casa de los Niños."

"We'll help you sort all of that out. Don't worry." Douglas was quick to try to reassure Tori.

What's going to happen to the kids without Silvia? Gigi's heart was pounding and she tried to stifle her fears. Douglas would help organize everything. She looked over at him now. He was very good in a crisis.

Gigi flashed back to the time with Arianna—at the end. Douglas had made sure that everything was in place, and he was the one who took care of all the details after her passing. But Gigi wasn't at all sure that this was a problem that could easily be fixed. Who could possibly do what Silvia had been doing for those kids?

"Honey."

Douglas's voice was pulling her away from her memories.

He grabbed for her hand. "Let's run back to pack up our things and talk to Loretta."

Gigi nodded. Douglas would see them through all of

this. She turned back to give Tori another quick hug. "We'll hurry back. Everything's going to be okay."

No, it isn't going to be okay. Silvia is gone. Gigi felt the lump in her throat as she turned to follow Douglas out of the cafe.

CHAPTER 28

The long ride from Antigua to the river had been a quiet one. The grief covered them all in the van like an unwanted blanket on a hot night. Gigi desperately wished that she could shrug it all away—that it had been a bad dream. But somehow the tragedy had happened, and now they needed to keep their focus on the children and what was going to be best for them. She let the tears come as her thoughts turned again to the faces of the kids and what they must be going through—Jimena, who had already lost her own mother. Gigi couldn't wait to take the small child into her arms.

"Tori?"

"Yes?" Tori turned around in her seat to face Gigi.

"How were the kids when you left? Do you think they're going to be okay?"

Tori seemed to be considering the question carefully before she replied. "Yes, they'll be okay. Some of them—the older kids—were taking it pretty hard, but they seemed to understand Silvia. She had never been shy about her faith with the children, so many of them believe that she's in heaven now. I think that's comforting for them, don't you?"

Gigi nodded, thinking back to the conversation with Jimena and Carlos when she first learned that Jimena's mother had passed away. "Yes, I'm sure that helps to explain things to the kids—to help them to process it all and to be able to get through their grief."

Douglas cleared his throat, and Gigi could tell that he had something on his mind. "What is it, darling?"

"I was wondering. I mean, I know it's only been a day but where is her body now? I hate to bring up such an unpleasant topic but will there be a funeral and how does that all work here? Do we need to contact people? Her family?"

Gigi thought that Douglas looked uncomfortable asking the questions, but it was like him to get right to the heart of the things that needed to be done, unpleasant or not. It was those types of things that he'd be sure to help Tori with.

"It's okay. I know we need to discuss these things and I'd rather do it now—before we get to the jungle—because I'd like for us to be able to focus on the kids once we arrive."

Douglas nodded for Tori to continue as he reached for Gigi's hand beside him.

"To answer your question, we've already buried her. Last night, shortly after it happened. It was deep in the jungle and it's what Silvia wanted."

Gigi tried not to let the shock show on her face as Tori continued.

"We found something—that Silvia had typed up. Well, a few of us knew it was there because she'd told us at different times—always in a joking sort of way."

"A will, you mean?" Douglas asked.

"Yes, I suppose. Although it was really Silvia just outlining her wishes—what to do if something happened to her." There were fresh tears falling down Tori's cheeks.

"That's good," Gigi said.

"Yes. She wanted to be buried deep in the jungle, and she'd also written that there was no family—no one to contact." Tori didn't hold back the sob that seemed to stick in her throat as she tried to continue. "She'd said that we were her family. The kids and those of us that knew her—truly knew her heart." She looked up at Gigi and Douglas now. "I know that you didn't know her long but she felt that way about you. She told me that the day you left—that you two were part of our family."

Tori's grinning caused Gigi to do the same, and she felt Douglas squeeze her hand.

"That makes me feel good. And we felt—and do feel the same way about you all," Gigi said.

"And of course we will do something with the children. There will be a ceremony tomorrow night." Tori smiled again as if remembering something. "Silvia wrote that she wanted the ceremony to be around the campfire with the kids—but that it should be a happy time, with music, dancing, and nice memories. I think the kids will like that, don't you?"

Gigi nodded her head. "Yes, I think they'll like that very much. And we can make it special for them—just how Silvia would have wanted it."

Gigi saw that Tori's smile faded quickly. She couldn't help but notice how stressed she looked. "Tori, it's going to be okay. We'll make sure of it."

"I know. But I just don't see how. I'm not really equipped to run things around there, and I don't really know of anyone else there who could do any better of a job. I mean, I know everyone will pitch in, but I think it's important to be realistic as we do go forward. And I do have to leave in the next week or so, even though the timing stinks. And I—I would just hate to see the orphanage shut—"

"Tori, that's not going to happen," Douglas was quick to interrupt. "Don't you worry about that. We'll figure everything out later, but I know that I can hire the help that you need. So let's not focus on that just now. We're going to help you get through this." He looked over at Gigi and squeezed her hand tight. "We're all going to get through this together."

CHAPTER 29

Gigi sat on the dock by the river with Jimena in her arms. They watched Douglas play in the water with Carlos and the older kids. She couldn't help but laugh as she saw the look on Carlos's face right before Douglas flung him far out into the water.

"Do you want to go in the water, honey?"

"Are you going to go in, Ms. Gi?"

"No, but I can sit here and watch you play." Gigi kissed the little girl on the top of the head.

"I want to sit here with you."

"Okay, then. That's just fine."

"Ms. Gi?"

"Yes?"

"Ms. Silvia is in heaven now with Mommy."

Gigi felt her words catch in her throat. "Yes, that's right. I bet she and your mommy are going to be great friends."

Jimena nodded. "Yes. I think so too. But I'm going to miss Ms. Silvia a whole lot."

Gigi felt her heart break that much more as she

hugged the little girl close to her chest. Jimena was crying now as Gigi held her, her own tears falling again.

"I know you will, honey. I'm really going to miss her too."

The two sat in silence. Jimena seemed on the verge of falling asleep and Gigi was lost in her thoughts as she watched Douglas and the kids in the river.

When they'd pulled up in the boat earlier, the children were on the dock to greet them, happy and welcoming, but Gigi could feel the heaviness that was their reality so soon after the accident. She longed to just scoop them all up and make everything okay with only hugs and kisses but she knew that it wasn't going to be so simple. There was grief to be felt and worked through. Gigi, as much as anyone, knew what it was like to lose someone. It would take time.

She wiped at another tear, noticing that Jimena had fallen asleep in her lap. She wondered how much time she and Douglas could take here. Could they really stay as long as Tori needed them to? They'd not had a moment alone to talk about any of their own travel plans, but Gigi guessed that they were on the same page in terms of making themselves available to help until Douglas could sort everything out. And she didn't doubt that he'd be able to.

She sighed, willing herself to just focus on taking it one step at a time right now. They'd only just arrived. She smiled as she thought about how they'd gotten so busy playing with the kids that they'd not even made it farther than the dock yet. She shifted a bit, causing Jimena to wake up in her lap.

"Oh, I'm sorry, honey. But we're probably going to need to go get ready for dinner soon."

The sun was rapidly setting; she noticed that Douglas was out of the water talking to Tori, who'd just walked up with Rafael by her side. The two of them made their way over to the dock, where Gigi was now getting up herself.

"We should probably go get settled," Gigi said to Douglas, who had an odd look on his face.

"Yeah. Honey, Tori had Rafael put our things in Silvia's hut—"

"—No, I don't want to stay there," Gigi interrupted.

She understood Tori's wanting to put them there. It was the nicest of all the living quarters on the property—not because Silvia had needed higher standards, but just because of the things that people had done for her over the course of the years that she'd lived there. She had seemed embarrassed when she'd given Gigi and Douglas the tour of her little hut, but Gigi had told her that she deserved it—that she should feel comfortable living in a place that she'd dedicated her entire life to.

"I'm sorry. Is that strange?" Tori looked worried now. "I didn't mean for it to be. I only want you two to be comfortable."

Gigi pulled Tori in for a quick hug. "No. I'm sorry. I shouldn't have reacted that way. It just caught me by surprise, that's all. I think I'd rather stay where we stayed before, if that's okay with you." She looked over at Douglas. "And if Douglas doesn't mind."

Tori and Douglas both nodded.

"That's kinda what I was thinking too," Douglas said. "I'll go with Rafael now and grab the bags and meet you over at the hut."

Gigi smiled when she saw the look on Carlos's face as he stood there listening to the conversation between the grown-ups.

"Can I come too? I can carry a suitcase because I've gotten a lot stronger now, Papa Doug."

Gigi thought the young boy's smile was wider than she'd ever seen it. His whole face had lit up when Douglas had stepped out of the boat earlier, and Gigi hadn't seen him leave her husband's side for a second.

Douglas reached down to put his hand on the boy's bicep, a playful look on his face. "My, you do seem a lot stronger. Yes. I think we do need your help, my friend. Thank you very much."

He headed down the dock with the two boys by his side, turning once to playfully blow Gigi a kiss. "See you in a few minutes, love."

Gigi blew a kiss back and then noticed that Tori had a funny smile on her face. "Oops. Too much?" Gigi laughed.

"No, not at all actually. I was just thinking how incredibly sweet you two are and also that it's kind of amazing for the kids to be around that actually, ya know? I mean they've not really had any kind of couples as role models in theirs lives, and so many of them don't even have a concept of what a loving and healthy relationship looks like."

Gigi let the words sink in before she responded. "You know, I think you have a good point there. Although maybe let's not mention that to my dear husband. He can go a bit overboard with the affection sometimes. It took me a bit to get used to."

Tori had a look of feigned shock on her face. "Oh, really?"

"Oh, you." Gigi swatted playfully at her friend's arm. "Nothing crazy. Just lots of kisses and hugs. And don't get me wrong, either. I'm not complaining at all about the affection. It was the public aspect of it that took some getting used to, but I don't really mind now." She was surprised to feel her face growing warm at what she guessed was a deep blush making its way across her cheeks.

Tori was laughing as she reached out to hug her friend. "Well, I think it's absolutely wonderful. You're a very lucky woman to have a man that loves you that much. And I think the two of you make an incredible team."

Gigi nodded, and for the first time that day, she felt happier tears in her eyes again.

CHAPTER 30

Gigi and Douglas were up early the next morning, anxious to meet Fernanda in the kitchen to help with the breakfast preparations. They'd had a good talk the night before, and Gigi now understood Douglas's plan to go back home to hire someone to come in and manage the orphanage. He knew a lot of people and he felt confident that he'd be able to get some feelers out that would land him some good candidates to interview.

Starting with telling Fernanda that morning, they intended to organize a meeting with everyone working there including the current volunteers.

The morning breakfast went well, busy as per normal, but Gigi felt the difference all the same. Silvia's absence was painfully obvious. It felt odd to be back without her there. And Gigi knew how much worse it had to be for the kids. They seemed to be mostly handling everything okay, but Gigi wondered about the stress they must be feeling and the effect that Silvia's loss would have on them.

She sighed as she started to get that feeling of being

overwhelmed herself, but she needed to remain strong for the kids. Regardless of her own grief and worry for them, she needed for them to feel safe and secure—that life was going to go on as they knew it there at the orphanage.

Her thoughts turned to one of the earliest conversations that she'd had with Silvia about the orphanage and the children. She'd said that her greatest mission was that it would be a home for them—a place where they would always feel safe and loved.

We have to keep that in mind above all else. Gigi really needed to be sure that Douglas was on the same page when it came to hiring someone to come in. He'd said that Gigi and Tori could be involved in the interviewing process also, so they'd do the best that they could. But who could ever take the place of Silvia? Gigi knew it wasn't possible.

She looked up now from where she was washing dishes to see Douglas walking towards her. He'd been on a mission since breakfast to have a quick chat with everyone—the doctor, teacher, gardener, all the staff and volunteers—to let them know about the meeting the next day. He was determined that they all needed to sit down together so that he could hear their views about what was needed, and also have a chance to express to them what his intentions were in going back to the States in just a few days.

"How's is going, hon?" Douglas gave Gigi a quick kiss on the cheek.

"All good here." Gigi looked at Carlos sitting nearby, his eyes ever watchful on Douglas. "And shouldn't you be in school, young man?" Gigi winked at him.

"I told him it was alright." Douglas looked a little sheepish. "He said that he really wanted to spend time with me this morning."

Gigi laughed. "Okay." And then she turned to Carlos. "But we can't make this a habit, you know."

Carlos nodded his head and grinned. "I know. Thank you very much. I think Papa Doug really needs my help today."

At that Douglas laughed and went to put his arm around the boy's shoulder. "And on that note—let's head out back to the garden. I want to see how the corn is coming along."

Gigi watched the two head off, marveling again at how Douglas had bonded with the small boy. He'd always been comfortable enough around Blu's girls and other children that they'd been around, but Gigi had never seen him this way before. It was very sweet and unexpected.

"Do you want to head over to check in with the younger kids? I know a little girl who will be very happy to see you." Tori's question interrupted Gigi's thoughts.

"Yes, I need to have a little snuggle with that gorgeous Gabriela."

Gigi didn't think she'd ever be able to hold her without remembering the first time she'd met her—the first time she'd met Silvia. It seemed so surreal—

everything that had happened in such a short time.

The two women headed over to the dorm that housed the younger children along with at least two other volunteers at one time, depending on how many children there were to look after. There were several kids that weren't old enough for the school program, but Tori had already shared that they were very fortunate to have more volunteers than normal at the moment—many of whom had agreed to stay on for a few weeks beyond what they'd originally planned for.

Things at the orphanage still seemed to be running pretty smoothly. Gigi was relieved to see that, and knew that it was largely due to Silvia's passion and the inspiration that she had instilled in those closest to her— those who had been working alongside her at the orphanage for years.

Everywhere Gigi looked on the grounds, she saw the hard work—the love—that Silvia had poured into the place, building it from the ground up, largely with her own hands. They'd find a way to continue everything she'd built here for the children. They'd find a way to honor her memory by continuing to provide a love-filled home for all of the kids who found their way to Casa de los Niños.

CHAPTER 31

Gigi sat by the fire, looking around at the faces of the children. The older kids were each holding a single candle. One of the girls kept a quiet beat on an old bongo drum and one of the older boys strummed a guitar as their sweet voices sang out the words to "Amazing Grace."

Gigi and Tori had loosely planned out the ceremony, and Tori had said that the hymn had been Silvia's favorite—one that she'd taught the children a long time ago.

Gigi looked over at Tori now and their eyes met through the tears that seemed to be overwhelming them both. Beside her, Douglas's arm came around her waist, the sound of his voice singing touching her.

Beside him stood Carlos, his eyes bright and his voice loud and clear, paying tribute to the woman he'd loved— the only mother he'd ever known. Gigi reached down to grab the hand Jimena was offering her, so small and fragile, yet completely trusting in her nature.

Somehow they'd do right by these kids—she and

Douglas. Gigi wasn't sure exactly how everything would play out, but she did know that with the money they had at their disposal, they could keep the orphanage running and keep the children cared for.

As the last chorus to the hymn rang out, Tori moved over near Gigi to hand Gabriela to her. Stepping forward, she spoke quietly, having the full attention of every child standing around the campfire.

"Tonight we are together here to honor our friend—"

"—and our mother," Rafael's voice called out, followed by the nodding of heads and the swipe at tears across faces by the kids in the crowd.

Tori smiled as she continued. "Yes, your mother as well. Ms. Silvia loved you all very much. You are her children and that will never change. Tonight is a time for remembering the good things about her, the things that you will not forget, the things that Ms. Silvia taught you. Anyone who would like to say a few words, please go ahead."

It was quiet around the campfire for a few minutes as the children's eyes darted around the circle.

Rafael cleared his throat and stepped forward just a little. "Ms. Silvia was my mother. I've been living here with her since I was two years old and she always told me not to forget that she loved me very much. Even though she is gone now, I think she is looking down on me from heaven."

He stepped back into the circle but Gigi thought he

looked like he still had something to say.

"Go on, Rafael," Douglas said. "It's okay. If you have something else to say, go ahead."

Rafael rubbed at his eyes quickly, a young man not quite comfortable showing his tears, Gigi thought; she watched as he squared his shoulders and took a deep breath.

"I just wanted to say that I—I never had a father either. But Ms. Silvia taught me how to be a man. She used to tell me that I was the man of our family and that I did such a good job helping and looking out for my brothers and sisters here."

Tori crossed over to give Rafael a hug that he didn't resist, and Gigi heard her quietly say the words that he was right about that—that he was the young man of their family.

Gigi was surprised to hear Jimena's voice speaking up quietly beside her, strong and sure of her words.

"Ms. Silvia is in heaven now with my Mommy and I'm glad that she will get to meet her." She looked up at Gigi as if for reassurance.

Gigi nodded her head and readjusted Gabriela in her arms in order to put one hand around Jimena's little shoulder as the girl continued.

"And I love Ms. Silvia very much," she finished.

The children took their time, with nearly every one having words to say about how they felt about the woman who had loved them—the woman who had raised them.

Tori came back over near Gigi at one point to take the sleeping Gabriela from her arms.

Gigi reached her free hand towards the one that Douglas offered her as he squeezed it before speaking to the group gathered.

"Gigi and I didn't know Ms. Silvia as long as you kids did, but the time we spent with her showed us a lot about who she was. The one thing that was made clear to both of us was just how much she loved each one of you—how very important you were to her." He looked at Gigi and squeezed her hand again before continuing. "We want you to know that everything is going to be okay. You kids will always be looked after here, and there will always be people here who love you and care about you."

Gigi didn't miss the swipe of her husband's hand across his eyes. She knew that he was feeling everything that she was feeling.

She realized in that moment—while paying tribute to a woman who had loved these children so passionately—that Silvia's passion had largely become her own—that somehow that felt like a gift to her now. Her eyes welled up with tears just thinking about it. It was like a gift from Silvia, herself. And Gigi thought back to the last conversation that she'd had with Silvia right before they'd left to go back to Antigua. Her eyes shining as if she'd known a secret, Silvia had told Gigi that she knew they'd be back—that she had a feeling she and Douglas would be back.

If only it had been under different circumstances; but they were back, and it was their duty not to leave without having things in place for the children who needed another special person in their lives to love them as much as Silvia had.

PAULA KAY

CHAPTER 32

Douglas had gathered everyone together in the dining area while most of the kids were in school, with the exception of several of the older kids who were minding the toddlers during the meeting so that the volunteers could all attend. Douglas had wanted everyone there to be able to freely speak about their needs and thoughts about what was best for the future of Casa de los Niños.

He started the meeting off by opening up a discussion about how the children had been doing the past few days. Everyone agreed that, for the most part, the kids seemed to be handling things very well. They would all continue to encourage them to talk freely about how they were feeling, even when they seemed to be okay from outward appearances. Gigi and Douglas knew better than anyone how easy it could be to mask feelings of grief, and it wasn't something that they wanted the children to have to go through without feeling that they always had someone that they could talk to.

Douglas waited until it was time to move on to the next subject at hand.

"Okay, next I'd like for each of you to speak about your area of expertise here at the orphanage and what things we need to know about what you will be needing help with. Fernanda, why don't we start with you?"

Fernanda had been at Casa de los Niños longer than anyone else sitting at the table, and she was the one who probably had known Silvia the best out of any of them. Gigi felt her pain at losing her friend. She could see it on her face now as the woman prepared herself to speak to the small group.

"I can run the kitchen just fine, and as long as I have at least a few volunteers helping me for an hour before and after each meal, I think I can manage. The area that Silvia has always been in charge of was the buying of the food that was needed, but I think I could handle that too as long as we get a good system in place." She looked towards Douglas. "And as long as the funds continue to be there."

Douglas nodded. "I want to say right up front that none of you have to concern yourself with the finances of running this place. This is something that Gigi and I can help with and we will do that—for whatever your needs are. And we'll be sure to get a budget in place for everything before we leave here."

They continued going around the table, each person talking about their position and what they felt was needed. All of the key people—the doctor, teacher, Fernanda in the kitchen, and the other staff members all agreed that they had no plans of leaving any time soon and certainly not within the next year, which was really the minimum level of commitment that Douglas had said would be ideal at this stage of their planning.

Gigi noticed that Tori hadn't spoken up yet, and she could tell by the look on her face that she might have something important to say.

"What's on your mind, Tori? Can you think of something that we're missing here?"

Tori looked like she was trying to choose her words carefully. "Well, from how I understand it, Douglas is basically going to pick from a handful of strangers—those most suited to running an organization?"

Douglas nodded his head, and Gigi already knew exactly where Tori's thoughts were leading.

"I don't know. I mean, I understand that I'm going to help with the interviewing and all of that. It's just so hard to imagine some random stranger coming in here to run the place." She looked at the others carefully. "Don't get me wrong. I'm extremely grateful that you two are here right now to help us figure this all out—I'm sure we all are. I don't even know what we'd do without you guys. It's just hard to imagine. That's all."

Douglas was nodding his head. "I do understand your concerns Tori. Really. It makes perfect sense." He reached for Gigi's hand under the table. "I'm afraid it's all we have right now. And not to put you on the spot at all, Tori, but you'd be everyone's first choice to take over for

Silvia, I think. But we do understand that you have things that you need to attend to—back home—so it's only sensible that we bring someone in who's qualified to do the job."

Tori was nodding her head, and Gigi saw her quickly wipe a tear away. "I know. It's just hard for me."

Gigi got up to go around the table to give her friend a hug. "We're going to get through this. And Douglas isn't going to bother bringing anyone over here who he doesn't genuinely feel will be a good fit for the kids— anyone who doesn't have a heart for this type of work."

"Yes, we can promise you all that." Douglas stood up from the table too, to walk over to put his arm around Gigi. "And of course we'll stay on for awhile also—a few weeks, a month or so—whatever's needed."

Gigi nodded her head in agreement as the meeting came to a close.

CHAPTER 33

Gigi felt Douglas's hand on her back as she sent off an email. She'd been up out of bed for a while at the small table in the room and was trying not to disturb him, but the space was small and she guessed that her lack of sleep had also kept her husband awake for most of the night.

"Are you okay, honey?"

"No, not really." Gigi turned her head to look her husband in the eye.

"Let's go back to bed and talk."

It was the only real space in the small room where they could both fit comfortably to have a conversation. Gigi had to smile because once again something small had brought up a memory of Silvia and their first meeting—in the hut—on the mattress.

"What's so funny?" Douglas smiled as he scooted over in the bed to make room for Gigi.

"Oh, I was just remembering the day we first met Silvia—the three of us in the bed having a nice chat."

"And with the baby." Douglas laughed too. He put

his hand behind her to rub her back gently while he spoke. "So you had a rough night sleeping?"

"Yes." She was trying to hold back tears.

"Do you want to talk about it?"

Gigi turned her head slightly to look at him. He was trying so hard to do the best that he could with the situation. She knew this.

"I'm just—oh, I don't know. I just feel very unsettled after our meeting with everyone last night."

Douglas was quiet for a few seconds; he seemed to be studying something across the room—gathering his thoughts before he spoke, Gigi thought.

"I know what you mean." He sighed and then looked over at her. "I'd be lying if I said that I wasn't feeling the same way."

Douglas reached for her hand. "I just—I don't know what else we can do, darling. I'm going to do my best to find the right person. You do know that, don't you?"

Gigi leaned over to kiss him on the lips. "Yes, of course I do, honey. I'm sure it will all work out. I think it's just so much to take in right now because it's still so raw."

Douglas nodded his head, but he didn't look reassured by her words.

"I do have some good news," Gigi said.

"I'd love some good news." He smiled. "What's that?"

"I got an email back from Lia today. She's going to

come—in just a few days. And she'll stay the entire time you're away and maybe a bit longer."

"That's terrific. I must admit, I'm a little surprised."

"Oh?"

"I assume you did tell her exactly how rugged it is around here?" Douglas laughed.

"Well, if we can handle it, I'm sure that Lia can too." Gigi smiled. "And yes, I did tell her that it was definitely not the Four Seasons here."

They both laughed.

"That's great. I'm glad she's coming."

"Yes, she's more than willing to roll her sleeves up to help. I have the feeling that Fernando won't mind sharing the kitchen with her. And if we can find the ingredients she needs, we can do some fun Italian-themed dinner nights around here."

"That sounds lovely. I'm really glad that she's able to get away from the restaurant."

"Yes, she said that it's pretty quiet in Tuscany right now—nothing that Carlo and Sofia can't handle. She tried to tell me that she was looking for a little adventure too, which of course cracked me up." Gigi saw the questioning look on Douglas's face. "Don't you think this has been quite an adventure for us, honey?"

Douglas planted a kiss firmly on her lips. "I think every day is an adventure with you, my love."

"Oh, you." Gigi laughed too as she kissed him back.

"I think we'd better make a move this morning. I'd

like to take one final walk around the entire property before I nail down our budget and best guess of a timeline for the work to be done. Which reminds me— they are going to be starting the new dormitory tomorrow. So I'll be here to get them started, but I'm going to be counting on you to oversee the project while I'm gone."

"Aye, aye, Captain." Gigi laughed, but she was feeling great joy that Douglas was trusting her with the project. They'd really learned a lot about working together as a team, and she quite enjoyed this new level that their relationship seemed to be on. "And can I join you on this walk, sir?"

Douglas brought her hand to his lips. "That would be my complete pleasure. Let's get going then, so we can be finished before breakfast."

Douglas opened the door of the small hut and practically stepped right into Carlos, who was sitting on the small porch with his face in his hands. The boy looked up at the sound of the door opening, a wide grin on his face.

"Buenos días, papa Doug." And he turned his head to yell in through the screen door. "Buenos días, Ms. Gi."

Gigi came out onto the porch laughing as she leaned down to give the boy a big hug. "Good morning, Carlos. My, you're up early."

"Si. I missed you." He directed this towards Douglas

as he reached his arms out to wrap around his waist.

Douglas laughed as he hugged the boy back. "I've not gone anywhere yet, silly."

Gigi thought he must have seen the same flash pass across Carlos's face as she did—a slight look of panic— until Douglas was quick to step off the porch, calling over his shoulder.

"Would you like to come with Gigi and me for a little walk?"

Carlos nodded his head, skipping up to fall in line with Douglas as he reached for his hand.

Gigi noticed that the boy was much more affectionate over the past few days than he had been prior to their saying goodbye before they'd left for Antigua. She thought it was very sweet but she knew that Carlos must also be feeling a lot of emotion about Silvia's passing.

The three walked along the path together, Douglas looking like he was deep in thought; he seemed to be eyeing the buildings along the way. They'd pretty much decided that starting with the dorms, all of the structures would be rebuilt from the ground up. They'd do it in stages, being strategic about moving the kids from building to building to handle their sleeping and schooling schedules.

Douglas had found a local contractor that he was very pleased with. He'd said that he had a very hard-working group of young men that could get a single building up within a week.

Douglas stopped in a clearing to sit down on a big log, pulling Gigi down beside him. They both sat in silence watching Carlos skip around, entertaining himself with a funny song that he loved to sing.

Douglas sighed and put his head down in his hands.

"What is it?" Gigi reached her hand up to rub his back, her leg pressed against his. She could practically feel the weariness—the sadness—that seemed to be coming from his entire body, and her heart broke that much more before her husband even answered her.

Douglas looked over at her. "I just—I can't help thinking—if only I would have had the guys out sooner working on the dorm—they would have been here to fix the roof."

"Douglas. Don't you dare blame yourself for that." Her hand went around his, squeezing it fiercely. "You heard Tori, the same as I did. If it wouldn't have been this time, it would have been something else that she'd have tried to do on her own. You couldn't have predicted a fall like that. No one thought that she would die from being on the roof."

He brought their clasped hands up to his lips to kiss Gigi's. "I know you're right, honey. I just feel so unsettled about it all." He looked her in the eyes. "Usually once I make a decision, that's it. This time... I don't know. I just don't know."

"I know what you mean. It's because there's so much sadness here in a place that was only a week ago filled with so much joy. I feel that too. It's awful and I want to fix it. I know you want to fix it too."

Douglas nodded his head and put his arm around Gigi's waist. "I do, honey. I just want to do right by the kids—and by Silvia."

Gigi gave him a quick kiss on the cheek. "You will. Everything's going to work out."

PAULA KAY

CHAPTER 34

Douglas and Gigi sat for a few more minutes in silence, Gigi hoping that Douglas could, in fact, let go of any guilt that he was feeling about Silvia's death. She needed for him to be okay—for them both to be okay. So much had happened, and she felt that they had changed. Both of them. Casa de los Niños—the children—had changed them.

They would do the best that they could to give the kids the best chance in the world to go on and make everything of their lives—everything that Silvia had wanted for each one of them.

Carlos ran up to them, interrupting her thoughts with his laughter as he hurled himself into Douglas's arms.

"Carlos."

The boy looked at Douglas.

"I'm going away for a few days."

"No."

The tears were instant, and she guessed that Douglas was as surprised as she was by the boy's strong reaction.

Carlos buried his face in Douglas's chest. "I don't

want you go." The sobs were coming fast now.

"Hey. Listen to me." Douglas was trying to get the boy to look at him. "I'm going to be coming back. And Gigi will still be here while I'm gone."

"That's right." Gigi leaned over to give Carlos a quick kiss on his forehead. "You're going to be just fine, and Douglas will be back again before you know it."

Carlos wiped the last of his tears away with a swipe of his hand and was quiet for several seconds; he seemed to be studying Douglas intently.

"Do you promise? Do you promise you'll come back?"

Douglas smiled and nodded. "Yes, buddy. I promise. I won't be gone long at all. Can we count on you to help with the little kids while I'm away?"

Carlos was nodding his head, his eyes not leaving Douglas's. He reached out his hands to put them on each side of Douglas's face. "Ti amo, Papa Doug."

Gigi's eyes instantly filled with tears as she witnessed the exchange in front of her. She could see the wetness in Douglas's eyes as he cleared his throat, looking like he was fighting to get words out.

He pulled the boy in for a hug and whispered, "I love you too, Carlos."

Gigi saw the tears and felt the emotion, raw and pure.

"Honey," she managed, reaching out her hand towards the boy. "You go help with breakfast now, okay? We'll be right along."

Carlos nodded and, with one look back over his shoulder and a wave, took off running towards the dining hall.

Douglas was crying beside her, his face in his hands, his whole body shaking. Gigi hadn't ever seen this much emotion in her husband, and it was almost more than she could bear. She reached her hand out to rub his back, her own tears falling silently as she waited for him to relax enough to speak.

Finally, after he'd been silent for several minutes, he turned his head to look at her, wiping away the last of his tears with his hand.

"Honey, what do you think about staying?"

Even as he spoke the words, Gigi saw his mood lift.

"Yes, of course. We'll stay to be sure everything is running smoothly. I thought we'd already decided that."

"No, that's not what I'm saying."

Gigi was confused.

"What do you mean? Sorry, I'm not following you, my dear husband." She laughed a little, trying to lighten the mood.

"I mean, I think we should stay. We should be the ones to run Casa de los Niños and look after the children."

Gigi felt herself looking at him as if he'd just said the strangest thing in the world to her, but slowly it registered and she felt her heart beating faster.

"Honey, are you serious?"

"As serious as I was the day I asked you to be my wife." He winked at her.

Gigi laughed at the memory of how sweet and nervous he'd been the day he proposed. She knew that Douglas didn't say things that he didn't mean. This seemed more spontaneous than normal, but she guessed that it had been on his mind the past few days.

He was standing now and pulling her to him for a hug. "I can see this being our life." He looked at her. "I mean, if it's something you want too."

"Yes." She laughed and hugged him back. "I'm just stunned. I can't believe you're saying this."

"I know. I never expected that I could be so taken— feel so invested—in these kids. And Carlos. Man, that little guy has my heart, ya know."

Gigi nodded, feeling the deepest love for her husband as she saw his eyes welling with tears once again at the mention of the little boy.

"And you're willing to give up your days of golf, then?" She winked, teasing him.

"Funny you should say that." Douglas laughed. "I was thinking that the kids really needed some type of sports program, and we do have this big clearing." He gestured beyond where they were sitting.

Gigi laughed. "That sounds like a brilliant idea— maybe after the buildings are finished."

"Of course." Douglas pulled Gigi in for a deep kiss. "Do you know how glad I am that you started this whole thing?"

"What, you mean with my constant nagging and depression?" She laughed, knowing exactly what he meant.

"I didn't even know that we needed something else in our lives, but you knew all along."

Gigi looked up into the eyes of the man she loved. "So, we're really going to do this, then?"

He smiled back at her, grinning widely. "We are."

She laughed. "You make me so happy."

He leaned over to kiss her again. "It's you that makes me happy. And don't you ever forget it."

They made their way hand-in-hand towards the dining hall, discussing what would happen over the next few weeks. They'd make the announcement to the children at dinner, after filling in Tori and the rest of the staff.

Douglas would keep his flight home as scheduled, but with the intention of taking care of a few personal matters and talking to a realtor about putting the house up for sale. There'd be a lot to do after that and Gigi would have to make a few trips back as well, but they both agreed that the most important thing was to get settled in with the kids. They were committed to making sure that the children knew that they were there to stay.

PAULA KAY

CHAPTER 35

Gigi and Lia sat in the small living room of what had been Silvia's place. Once Gigi and Douglas had made the announcement that they were staying, Tori had insisted that they made the move into the bigger space, and there hadn't been a reason to resist. Gigi felt quite sure that Silvia's blessing was all over the decisions they were making, and now it gave her a great sense of peace to be in the space that she knew Silvia had enjoyed so much.

Lia had fallen in love with baby Gabriela from the moment she saw her, and was holding her now as the two women talked. Lia had been there for a week, and the two friends had developed an easy pattern of working alongside one another at Casa de los Niños. Gigi had been right in thinking that Lia wouldn't have any issues with the ruggedness of the place and that she'd fall for the kids just as Gigi and Douglas had done.

Gigi looked at her friend and grinned.

"You know, Gabriela is one of the few children here that is adoptable."

Lia looked over at her and laughed. "Oh, really? You

don't think I'm too old to start raising kids?"

Gigi looked at her friend as she chose her words carefully. "I'm only partly joking, you know."

Lia laughed. "Well, we'll have to see what Antonio thinks about that. It's certainly not been anything we've ever talked about but—well, who knows? Stranger things have happened, I suppose." She leaned down to kiss Gabriela on the nose as the child giggled in her arms.

"Speaking of Antonio…" Gigi could hardly believe that in just a few days everyone that she loved would be there in the jungle of Guatemala with her. It was a rather surreal feeling, to say the least.

Lia grinned. "Antonio's arriving on Friday. And I spoke to Blu also. They'll be in on Saturday."

"I still can't believe that everyone is coming. Douglas will be so surprised," Gigi said.

Douglas was due back tomorrow, and Gigi had let him know that Lia had decided to stay on for the ribbon-cutting ceremony and party that they were having on Sunday for the building dedication. The men had finished it up the day before and Gigi had been over the moon with how well it had turned out. She couldn't wait for Douglas to see it.

Lia laughed. "Seriously, Gigi, I really can't believe that you two are doing this. I'm incredibly happy for you. We all are." She reached for Gigi's hand, and Gigi caught a look of something on her friend's face.

"What is it? That look?" She laughed, knowing her

friend well.

"Well, I knew you'd be okay. I really did." Lia laughed. "But I really can't believe the change I'm seeing in you. I mean, I can remember speaking to you not so many weeks ago and—well, it's just really incredible how quickly things can change, isn't it?"

Gigi reached over to hug her friend. "And I know that you know a thing or two about that also. But yes, you're right. I feel like a different person, and dare I say that I don't know that I've ever been happier." Gigi felt a lump form in her throat. "And Lia, wait until you see Douglas—with the kids, I mean. He's really incredible."

Lia smiled. "I can't wait to see him—and the both of you in action around here."

PAULA KAY

CHAPTER 36

Everyone gathered close to the porch of the new dormitory where Gigi, Douglas, and Tori stood in front of the big ribbon that they'd placed across the front door. The children had been mesmerized by it and the new building, and Gigi guessed that they were more than curious to see the new place where they'd be sleeping. All of the older kids had agreed that they wanted to wait for Douglas to return before they saw it. And they wanted to throw a big party.

Gigi smiled, thinking about her earlier discussions with the kids. Any excuse to throw a party and they were all over it. But she had to admit it was a fun thing to do before everyone had to return home. Gigi loved it that Blu and Lia had a chance to see the children happy—the way that Gigi and Douglas had known them to be.

Her attention was brought back to the ceremony as the voices of the children singing "Amazing Grace" rang out. They had insisted that it was the best way to start— that Ms. Silvia would have wanted it that way.

Gigi felt Douglas's hand reach for her own as they

finished singing the hymn and he cleared his throat to make the little speech that he'd prepared.

Originally Gigi had thought that the building should be built in Arianna's honor, but after everything that had happened—after losing Silvia—the kids' new dormitory was officially named la Casa de Silvia. Gigi smiled thinking about it. The orphanage would always be Silvia's home; the kids would always be her children. Her picture hung just inside the doorway; her memory would be kept alive by all the kids who slept here.

And outside, on the porch, sat a single bench made of wood—it was there in honor of Arianna and everything she'd done—everything her gift of money had done—for the children and this beautiful place that Gigi and Douglas would now call their home too.

The clapping and shouting from the children interrupted her thoughts as she focused her attention on Douglas's speech and the big ribbon across the door.

"You do it, honey," Douglas whispered to her.

Gigi cut the ribbon and the crowd erupted in more clapping and a sea of smiles from the kids now making their way up the porch steps.

Douglas led the excited children through the doors and inside for their first look at their new home.

Jemma had made her way up the steps to stand next to Gigi, and Gigi took her hand to lead her over to the bench for a chat. She'd hardly had time to speak with her and was dying for a chat with the young girl.

"How's it going, my lovely girl?"

Jemma grinned. "I like it when you call me that. But I think Mom would argue that I'm not always so lovely." She laughed.

"Oh, I'm not so sure about that. I happen to know that your mom thinks you're pretty terrific."

"What's that? My ears are burning." Blu came up beside them with Lia following right after her.

Gigi pulled the resistant Jemma onto her lap to make room for the other two women to sit beside them.

"Gigi, I'm too big to sit on your lap." Jemma giggled.

"You are never too big for a cuddle, my darling." Gigi laughed and kissed the young girl on the cheek, Jemma finally becoming still and putting her head back against Gigi's chest.

Gigi noticed Lia's fingers gently tracing over the small gold plate along the top of the bench. In loving memory of Arianna, it read.

"I can't believe it's been five years," Blu said and seemed to be watching the expression on Lia's face.

"I know. It's hard to believe how much has happened, isn't it?" Lia smiled when she asked the question.

"Five years since what?" Jemma asked, sitting up a bit in Gigi's lap.

"Five years since Arianna passed away, honey," Gigi answered.

"Oh." Jemma seemed thoughtful. "Mom?"

"Yes." Blu said.

"Do you think Ari would have liked it here? Do you think she would have liked all the kids?"

Blu grinned. "Well, she sure did like you a whole lot, didn't she?"

Lia reached across Blu's lap to grab Jemma's hand for a quick squeeze. "Ari talked about you all the time. Do you remember—that she always called you J-bean?"

Jemma giggled. "I forgot that she called me that. I still really like jelly beans." She paused for a second, as she settled her head back against Gigi's chest. "I think Ari loved me. I think I remember that."

Gigi felt her eyes tear up as she kissed the top of Jemma's head. "That she did, my lovely girl. She loved you a whole lot."

And as Gigi looked over at Blu and Lia sitting beside her smiling, she was reminded once again of how extremely fortunate she'd been to have inherited this little family of hers. And she guessed that Arianna could have never known that it was by far the greatest gift of anything that she'd given to Gigi.

CHAPTER 37

Gigi stood off to the side of the dance floor, Douglas's arm around her and Jimena sitting nearby. She couldn't help but laugh as she watched Rafael showing Jemma his dance moves.

Jemma's attitude had been surprisingly great the whole time that they'd been there. Gigi really hadn't known what to expect from the little girl, but she'd joined right in with the kids, playing and helping with the younger children.

Gigi nudged Douglas and gestured out towards the dance floor. "Look at Antonio and Lia. Have you ever seen anything so sweet?"

The couple were dancing to a song with Gabriela in Antonio's arms and giggling as he swung her around in time to the music.

"Stranger things have happened, alright." Gigi said under her breath, laughing.

"What's that, honey?"

"Oh just something Lia had said the other day."

Douglas laughed, kissing her on the cheek. "There's no telling what you two ladies are up to while I'm away."

Gigi grinned back.

"I can't believe how big Kylie's gotten."

Gigi watched Blu's youngest daughter take a few tentative steps between Chase and one of the older girls, laughing and looking quite proud of her newfound skill.

"What are you two lovebirds whispering about over here?" Blu came up beside them.

"Oh, we're just so happy that you guys were able to make it." Gigi reached out to give her friend a big hug. "It really means a lot to us."

"Are you kidding? I wouldn't have missed it—none of us would." Blu leaned in to give Gigi a quick kiss on the cheek. "You two are our family. And that's not going to change just because you're now halfway across the world."

Douglas laughed. "Okay, so that's a very big exaggeration, but it's probably a slightly longer flight than between San Francisco and San Diego."

"Oh, I'm only joking." Blu grinned. "I do hope that you'll still come back to visit and make the annual trip to Italy."

Gigi laughed. "Oh, are we doing an annual trip to Lia's now?"

"Indeed." Blu laughed. "I've been working too hard. Chase has insisted that I put our yearly vacation plans on the calendar—in marker."

Gigi and Douglas looked at one another and laughed.

"That's a good man you've got there." Douglas winked.

"Yep, he's a keeper alright."

"Well, you're more than welcome to come here to stay any time, although I can't really promise that it will be a vacation—at least not one that doesn't include some work." Gigi winked.

"I'll keep that in mind."

Gigi followed Blu's gaze to where Jemma was dancing with a few of the older kids.

"I must admit that Jemma seems to fit right in here, which is a bit of a shock." Blu laughed.

"Yes, Douglas and I were commenting on that as well. You know, if it ever worked out—" Gigi glanced at Douglas, who was nodding his head and smiling—his permission for her to continue. "—we could keep Jemma here for a summer."

Blu grinned. "That we might have to consider. I'd miss her terribly, but maybe it would be good for her." Blu leaned over to give Gigi another quick hug. "And on that note, I better go see if Jemma's had anything to eat. I haven't seen her stop dancing all night."

Gigi felt Douglas's arm around her waist once again, and she thought maybe she'd never felt so content in all her life. The only thing that could have possibly made the occasion that much sweeter would have been having Arianna here with them all, but even as she had the thought, there was a small voice in the back of her mind, reminding her that just maybe everything was as it was meant to be…just the way it was.

She noticed the big smile on Douglas's face as he watched all of the kids on the dance floor; they laughed and stopped to wave whenever they saw that they had his attention.

Carlos and Jimena, hand-in-hand, ran up to where they stood.

"Come dance with us, Papa Doug, Ms. Gi." Carlos was grinning widely at Gigi, who laughed in response.

Jimena was tugging on Douglas's pants leg, looking a bit more shy than was normal. "Papa Doug, will you pick me up?"

Gigi and Douglas looked at one another and grinned. Douglas scooped the little girl up with one arm and took Gigi by the hand with the other as they made their way out onto the dance floor, to the delight and cheers of all the children dancing around them.

Douglas leaned over to whisper in Gigi's ear. "Honey, I think it's fitting to say that by some miracle we have our children after all."

Gigi nodded, wiping away the tears that she couldn't hold back—tears of pure joy—for this new family that somehow they'd found and now had the privilege to be a part of.

Yes, everything was just as it should be.

ABOUT THE AUTHOR

Paula Kay spent her childhood in a small town alongside the Mississippi River in Wisconsin. (Go Packers!) As a child, she used to climb the bluffs and stare out across the mighty river—dreaming of far away lands and adventures.

Today, by some great miracle (and a lot of determination) she is able to travel, write and live in multiple locations, always grateful for the opportunity to meet new people and experience new cultures.

She enjoys Christian music, long chats with friends, reading (and writing) books that make her cry and just a tad too much reality TV.

Paula loves to hear from her readers and can be contacted via her website where you can also download a complimentary book of short stories.

PaulaKayBooks.com